MURDER IN LIMA

KURT HAMMER BOOK 2

MATS VEDERHUS

Copyright (C) 2016 Mats Vederhus

Layout design and Copyright (C) 2019 by Next Chapter

Published 2019 by Terminal Velocity – A Next Chapter Imprint

Edited by Emily Fuggetta

Cover art by Cover Mint

This book is a work of fiction. Names, characters, places, and incidents are the product of the author's imagination or are used fictitiously. Any resemblance to actual events, locales, or persons, living or dead, is purely coincidental.

All rights reserved. No part of this book may be reproduced or transmitted in any form or by any means, electronic or mechanical, including photocopying, recording, or by any information storage and retrieval system, without the author's permission.

To
Sara Marie, for life
Sunniva, one of the strongest persons I know
Agatha, for a lifelong love of crime and mysteries

PROLOGUE

The black Mercedes Maybach Pullman pulled up in the middle of New Bond Street, under an ashen sky. Raining cats and dogs, the weather gods were clearly in an extra bad mood this day—even for London. A man wearing a black bowler hat and coat stepped out from the driver's seat, closed the door behind him, and with firm steps went to the rearmost door located almost five meters to the rear. When he opened the door, the man bowed and said, "Welcome, sir!"

Cars such as a Rolls Royce Phantom, Porsche Panamera 4, and Aston Martin DB9 occupied all the parking spaces along the narrow street. People who hadn't barricaded themselves indoors to escape the rain stood in small clusters on each side of the street, pointing and whispering amongst themselves, apparently just as curious as the journalists from all over the world who had shown up and were now preparing to assault the newly arrived car.

"Thanks!" the man answered, getting out of the car.

His skin was lightly tanned, and he had black, curly hair which lay in a nice bun on the top of his head. Underneath his light brown leather jacket, he wore a dark blue turtleneck and an orange T-shirt. A green cotton scarf was wrapped around his throat. On the tip of his nose sat glasses with thick, black frames.

An explosion of flashes assaulted him as the journalists screamed at the top of their lungs.

"No comment," said the man firmly as he ran from the car toward the two display windows of the marble building. He moved with confident steps and a strutting neck to a creamy white façade.

Golden letters spelling the name "Sotheby's" filled the space between the second and third floor. The entrance to Sotheby's auction house was comprised of black, stately doors with golden handles. As he stood outside, he was met by a tall man dressed in a black coat and top hat.

"Please hurry up, sir," he said. "The auction starts in five minutes."

"Thanks. I assume that I have a reserved seat," answered the man with the green scarf.

"Of course." The tall man opened one of the black doors. "Welcome!"

NEW RECORD AT AUCTION
BY FELICIA ALVDAL AND FRANK HANSEN

The paintings, *Several Circles* and *Autumn in Bavaria*, by the Russian artist Vasily Kandinsky (1866 – 1944) were sold this weekend for respectively 15 and 18.9 million pounds at the auction house Sotheby's in London.

"Kandinsky was a very popular artist, and I expected that these would be sold for a lot. We are still overwhelmed by the result," auctioneer David Bennett said to NTB this weekend.

Record

Several Circles beat the record of a painting selling for eleven million pounds. This record was then beaten again by the sale of *Autumn in Bavaria*. A bidding war ensued between an unknown Russian buyer and the controversial Norwegian billionaire John Fredly.

Fredly's press secretary, Hans Eriksen, stated to NTB, "John Fredly has been interested in art for his entire life, and Kandinsky is his favorite artist. The fact that the price he paid for these works was a record high is just a footnote in the big scheme of things."

Uncertain

Questioned about whether or not Fredly could imagine lending the paintings to a museum to share the works with a larger audience, he answered, "This is something he's not yet considered. It isn't impossible that it will happen in the future, but then it'll most likely be in a Peruvian museum in Lima, where he lives."

The Russian buyer wouldn't be identified but said via his press secretary, "We are very disappointed by the result. Kandinsky is a part of Russian national history and doesn't belong in South America. We are willing to pay Fredly twice what he paid over ten years if he agrees to sell, and we've informed him of this."

Not going to happen

For Fredly, however, this is unacceptable.

"Fredly will be keeping the paintings in his home in Lima, Peru, for the foreseeable future, where he will be enjoying them together with family and guests," Eriksen concluded.

1

19 JULY 2014

Kurt Hammer staggered out of a black and white chess-patterned taxi in the Miraflores area of Lima, Peru.

He went around the car to the driver's side, before remembering that he had already paid, and continued crossing the street, ignoring the traffic signal in front of him. From the driver's seat of his taxi, Juan Pablo looked on with eyes like saucers.

Oh my God, he will be hit, Juan thought before opening the door and running out to grab hold of his foreign client's arm. Compared to the gangly Norwegian, whose head was almost two meters above the ground, Juan Pablo looked more like a child than a taxi driver.

"Hey, man, where do you live?" Juan Pablo spoke as calmly as he could and in English. The words exited his mouth with a slight Quechuan accent.

Kurt pointed to a red building across street. At the bottom it said "Ibero Librerias" on a blue background. Between two rows of big windows, in the middle of the building, were the words "Pariwana Backpackers" in white lettering.

Juan Pablo put his arm around his tall, foreign client, who suspiciously resembled some American actor. *Who was it ... Jeff Bridges!* He had the same thin frame, blue eyes, slightly sunken face, and sharp chin covered in a beard. His hair was dark blond, greasy, and touched his shoulders. This Norwegian's nose was crooked from several fights over the years——a fact Juan Pablo didn't find curious in the least, considering how the man drank. He hoped that someone inside would take care of his client so the taxi driver could go back to work. The odd couple was almost run over twice by a green bus and a blue Range Rover as they attempted to cross the street.

Finally, they came to a black door, which was located under a black sign with yellow letters that read "Pariwana." Juan discovered a red button on his left-hand side and pushed it. After one minute the door opened.

Juan sighed heavily when he pushed the door open and noticed a stairway.

20 July 2014

Kurt Hammer woke up at 11:31 a.m. the next day. His head felt like a water balloon about to burst. *What happened yesterday?* he thought.

Kurt had no clue, but when he realized that he'd eventually fallen asleep in his own bed, a satisfied little smile spread across his lips. Slowly but surely, he opened his eyes and then looked around the room. It was covered with red wallpaper and sparsely furnished. Except for the double bed fashioned from dark wood and two nightstands, it contained nothing but a closet. When he turned his head, he almost lost his breath. Lying beside him in the bed was a Peruvian woman in her late twenties. She had long, jet-black hair, which touched her shoulders, as well as bangs. Her big lips were still painted red from the night before. Kurt noticed, too, that she had a fairly long scar over her right eye.

Kurt lightly touched her naked shoulder.

She opened her eyes slowly. Then she turned around and looked up at Kurt. Under a couple of thick but manicured brows were almond shaped eyes with pupils like coffee beans.

"Madre de dios," she cried. *Mother of God!*

She jumped out of bed, dragging the bedsheet she used to cover her breasts.

"What happened yesterday?" she asked.

"I had hoped that you could give me the answer to that," Kurt replied.

"Are you used to waking up with strange women by your side?"

"Hmm. It's been a while, but it's happened. Who are you?" Kurt smiled carefully.

"I'm Sara Sofia Ulo. I went out with friends last night, and ... Madre de dios! They must be wondering where I went. Do you have a telephone I can borrow?"

"Don't you have your own?"

"I lent it to my friend last night before I blacked out."

"I see ..." Kurt reached over to the nightstand, grabbed his iPhone 5s, and handed it to her.

"Thanks," she said and sat down on the edge of the bed with her back to him.

After a couple of minutes, she concluded that her friend wouldn't pick up the telephone.

"Fuck it, I'll send her a message," she said.

Finally, she handed the cell phone to Kurt and started to dress.

Sara Sofia put on a short black skirt, long black leather boots, and a red corset.

"Thanks for a nice night, which I cannot remember anything of." As she was about to close door behind her, she turned and said, "Next time, you better remember that in this country the men always open the door for the ladies." She winked.

Well, that was awkward. I'll never drink again, Kurt thought after she'd left.

He crawled out of the bed, but when he tried getting up, it felt like the room was located in a ship trapped in a hurricane. After spending five minutes finding his balance, he grabbed his black toiletry bag and carried it to the bathroom across the hallway.

There he was met by the hostel's overeager activity leader. The little Colombian barely came up to Kurt's shoulders and looked at him with wide-open eyes, which seemed like two big coffee beans in the nonplussed face.

"Kurt! Where were you yesterday? I heard that they had to carry you into the room," he said.

"No worries. I was just a little drunk and decided to go home early," said Kurt.

"You ought to shave. And take a painkiller ... or five. Your eyes are bloodshot. Good thing no one looked for you," said the activity leader.

Kurt was too tired to search for the possible sarcasm in his voice. He, instead, turned his back so he could face the mirrors above a row of wash basins. He hated being told what he should or shouldn't do. The little prick was still right about one thing, though: his beard, and hair for that matter, could use a trim. His ordinarily shoulder-length, dark blond hair was a rat's nest, and his beard was overly long and bushy.

Kurt decided to take drastic measures. During the next fifteen minutes, he trimmed his hair to a couple of millimeters and shaped his bushy beard into a handsome sailor's beard. Then he quickly downed a couple of aspirin.

A couple of hours later, Kurt Hammer stood on the first floor of the big clothing store, Ripley, at Dean Valdivia 577, looking around. All of a sudden, he heard a male voice behind him talking in Norwegian.

"Aren't you ... Kurt Hammer?" said the man.

The man standing before Kurt looked to be in his forties, with short, dark hair and square glasses framing a round face. His eyes were blue with thin brows arched over blue eyes. His dark Armani suit was immaculate, but he was missing the little finger on his right hand.

Trying to place the man, Kurt raised one brow. After a half minute he had to concede. "Who are you?" asked Kurt.

The man stretched out his hand with a smile. "Hugo Friis. I read about you in VG and Aftenbladet last year, you see. My employer subscribes to them. You must be a celebrity in Norway now," he said.

Kurt smiled carefully. "That may be so, but people mostly keep quiet around me. Accident at work?" Kurt pointed at Hugo's right hand.

"Oh, yeah. I used to work as a fisherman outside Harstad, where I come from. What are you doing here?" asked Hugo.

"I needed a vacation. A colleague and friend recommended I travel far away, and my therapist said it would be a good test for me to travel to a place with cheap alcohol. But that's a long story ... and what are you doing here? Or more importantly ... who are you working for?"

Hugo Friis smiled playfully. "An old acquaintance. Funnily enough, he's hosting a dinner for friends tonight. I think he would appreciate if you showed up," he said.

"Ahh ..." Kurt was reluctant to answer.

"Trust me, you won't regret it! Have you heard about Huaca Pucllana?" asked Hugo.

"No ..." said Kurt.

"It is a big excavation project in Miraflores, where Lima Incas built pyramids. Come at 8:00 precisely," said Hugo.

The man took out a brochure from the pocket of his suit. It pictured something built with primitive bricks, which resembled a cliff. In the right corner it said "Huaca Pucllana" in white lettering, followed by "the temple of the worshippers of the sea" in yellow lettering.

"Who is this acquaintance, then?" asked Kurt.

"You'll know if you show up! And..." Hugo scrutinized him from top to bottom. Kurt was wearing a canary-yellow suit, a light brown fedora, and red sailor's slippers "... see if you can find a suitable dinner suit, for God's sake," he said.

With that, the man turned and disappeared to a different section of the clothing store.

What a rude thing to say, Kurt thought and walked back to look for Hawaiian shirts and sunglasses, despite the fact that Lima hardly ever saw any sun. The months of January to April saw an average temperature of twenty-two degrees Celsius, something which suited Kurt well.

―――

At 7:30, Kurt changed into sandals and a Hawaiian shirt. He lay on the Pariwana hostel's roof with earbuds in and a Marlboro gold hanging out of his mouth while reading *Fallen Angels* by Gunnar Staalesen. All of a sudden, he was shocked to life by someone touching his shoulder. The little Colombian he'd met earlier stood by his side.

"Kurt, Kurt, Kurt," said the man.

"What is it, Jose?" said Kurt.

"There's a man for you in the reception. He says he's there to pick you up."

"Huh? I haven't ordered a taxi," said Kurt.

"I think you should come take a look," said the man.

"Okay," said Kurt.

Kurt reluctantly stood up, noticing that it was almost dark outside and praised Gunnar Staalesen for occupying him for most of the day. A big gang with huge knapsacks on their backs stood, as per usual, in the white reception area on the second floor; they were in the process of checking in. Behind them stood a small man in a black uniform with a driver's hat on his head.

"Kurt Hammer?" he asked when Kurt came into the reception via the broad staircase which led to the roof.

"That's me," answered Kurt.

Kurt noticed the several surprised stares when he spoke to the little man.

"I have been instructed to drive you to Huaca Pucllava," said the man.

"How did you know where I lived?" asked Kurt.

The man smiled. "My boss knows perfectly well who you are," answered the man.

"Ahh, and who is he?" asked Kurt.

"Join me and you'll see," said the man.

Kurt had started to tire of the secrecy around this employer but followed when the little the man started moving towards another staircase which led down to the street level.

The largest car Kurt had ever seen was parked by the

street: a black Mercedes Maybach Pullman, which was about six meters long. Kurt started to understand that the list of people he knew who could arrange this kind of dinner just grew significantly shorter. Still, he had no idea who it could be. The little man opened the rearmost door and signaled that Kurt should get inside.

The car had upholstered seats, and an open bottle of Pahlmeyer Napa Valley Chardonnay waited for him between the two rearmost seats. Kurt immediately started sweating. *I deserve half a glass,* he thought. Right afterward, the image of Felicia's icy blue eyes filled his mind, along with the smell of Chanel No. 5 mixed with the guilt and shock he'd felt when he woke up that morning. "What a fucking idiot you are, Hammer," he said to himself, opened the window, and poured the contents of the bottle out across the asphalt like a seventy-dollar rain shower. Under Lima's constantly foggy sky, the cars filled the roadway, and Kurt wondered for how long they would be driving. They arrived fifteen minutes later.

Shaking, Kurt opened the car door, only to see oblong pyramids in front of him. They seemed to be made from … sand?! He didn't understand how that was possible in the middle of this big city. Before he had the time to scratch his beard, a man walked out of the entrance between the fence, which surrounded the place, and came over to him.

The man was wearing a green scarf and a light brown leather jacket. His hair was black and curly, fashioned into a nice bun at the top of his head. Kurt's jaw dropped.

"It's John?" asked Kurt.

"The one and only," the man answered and beamed.

"I realized that you'd become someone big after university, see," said Kurt and gave his old friend a big hug, reminiscing about their time together in Bodø.

A party for the new students, arranged by the eldest prefect at the Police Academy, had resulted in forty-seven people being squeezed into one and a half floors of an old house from the fifties at Mørkved, just outside the center of town. The couches had to have been five years old. The walls were plastered with pictures of Wham! and Ole I'Dole. The eldest prefect had bought A-ha on vinyl, and to this day Kurt could still remember the lyrics of "The Living Daylights."

During the night, Kurt had tried his luck with Marta with the big boobs, the punk Camilla, and Ragnhild with the pigtails. He was more or less brutally rejected by all of them, but things didn't turn really sour until he made out with the eldest prefect's broad. Kurt was thrown out into minus-fifteen-degrees Celsius weather. On his way home, he managed to fall asleep in a mound of snow. Out of the blue, John Fredly, his old classmate from Trondheim, appeared like a shadow in the night. He had to practically carry him home on his strong shoulders and helped get him to bed.

THE NEXT DAY, Kurt had made up his mind about starting a regular training regimen. He was out of shape and knew it, realizing that it was a miracle he had passed the physical examinations for the Police Academy. For the next three months, the pair worked out two or three times a week.

"You helped me become a better policeman," said Kurt.

"How so?" John asked, beaming at him at him with a funny smile.

"If you hadn't saved my life in the mound of snow that night, I never would have realized how out of shape I was and started working out."

"Haha, I didn't save your life, but you probably would have gotten serious frostbite." John friendly across his back.

"Sorry for what happened after," said Kurt.

"Don't think about it. We ... didn't turn out so well," John said and sighed.

"What are you doing here?" said Kurt.

"Well, maybe you heard that I became a tax refugee a few years back. First I moved to Colombia and then here. I came over for this project, which I wanted to invest in and keep a closer eye on," said John.

"Really? And what's going on here? Digging?" asked Kurt.

"Not just any digging. Lima was founded in a desert, Kurt. The Incas built pyramids here, where they sacrificed and buried young women and babies," answered John.

Kurt scratched his beard. "Interesting! So, you're into charity in your older years?"

John Fredly laughed the short, snorting laughter which was customary for him.

"Well, I'm still into shipping, even if most of the money comes from fish farming nowadays. We actually do a lot of exporting to Lima and Peru," he explained.

Kurt lit up. "Then all the ceviche I've been eating down here has been Norwegian fish!"

John grinned. "Some of it, at least. Speaking of, please join me inside. Let's eat," said John.

John showed the way to the entrance, and Kurt followed him.

"What's the occasion?" asked Kurt.

"I've collected more art for my personal collection. I thought we could eat here because the surroundings are magical," John answered.

He was right about that, thought Kurt. The pyramids

stood almost six meters tall, surrounded by Inca buildings, complete with life-size models of Incas in contemporary costumes. When they walked past the ticket office inside the fenced-in area, they took to the right and were welcomed by Hugo Friis, who was wearing a gray Armani suit and white dress shirt. Kurt, a man who spent extremely little time on his own appearance, couldn't help staring at the suit which he knew had to have cost at least two to three thousand dollars. Hugo Friis, fortunately, chose not to comment on it.

"Welcome to Huaca Pucllava," Hugo said with a smile. "I'm the waiter for the evening. Take a seat in the restaurant and make yourselves at home."

"Thanks," said Kurt.

As they entered the restaurant, which resembled a veranda, Kurt discovered why the myth of the Incan city of gold existed. The floodlights surrounding the pyramids made it look as though they were made of gold.

A long table covered in a white tablecloth was set up on the veranda. Several people were already sitting around the table. Kurt recognized some of them, but others he'd never seen. An attractive blonde dressed in a tight-fitting, black dress sat on one of the sides. To her right was a short man in a black suit. Kurt recognized him as the king of hotels, Jarle Sørdalen, and his wife, Anastasia. The short man immediately got up and came to them.

"I see you've made a new friend," he said to John and beamed.

"Kurt Hammer is actually one of my oldest friends. We attended secondary school together and studied in the same city," he said.

"Jarle," said the man and held out a hand to Kurt.

Kurt noticed that he was wearing black leather gloves.

"Kurt Hammer. Any particular reason you are wearing gloves in this climate?" Kurt smiled.

Suddenly, a light appeared in Jarle's eyes. "Mysophobia. Quite frankly, I don't like germs. You're that journalist who was fired by NCIS, isn't that correct? And almost died when Trondheim Torg was blown to smithereens."

"Yeah," said Kurt, smiling apologetically.

"Jarle is a friend and business partner," John added.

"Come on, we're best friends, aren't we?" Jarle put an arm around John's back.

"Yeah," answered John, clearly bothered. "Let's sit down?"

"Yeah, let's," Kurt answered and rubbed his hands together.

John settled down on the opposite side, next to a lady with red hair, who looked like she could be in her sixties. She was wearing a purple dress and a dark, broad-brimmed hat with feathers.

"This is Rebecca Swanson," John said to Kurt. "She is a tax refugee from England."

Kurt settled down at her left side.

"We met through a mutual hatred of tax authorities," John continued.

"I see," Kurt answered. "Nice to meet you." Kurt stretched out a hand.

"You too," she said, shaking his hand. Her eyes shone like two green gems.

"Rebecca, this is Kurt Hammer. He is a famous Norwegian journalist and will probably tell us the dramatic story of how he ended up here."

Kurt sighed. *This will be a long night,* he thought.

"Can't wait," Rebecca said and smiled.

At the sound of someone briskly walking up behind them, Kurt, Rebecca, and John all turned around.

"Ah, friends, this is Karl Homme," exclaimed John and immediately got up.

The man seemed to be nearly two meters tall and was tanned, with long, brown hair which he kept in a man-bun. He wore a black fedora, and Ray-Ban sunglasses covered his eyes. The cream-colored suit from Dolce & Gabbana contrasted sharply with his beard and mustache. A brown leather bag hung from his shoulder, and he held up a hand to wave. Around his right wrist was an Omega Seamaster watch.

"As you probably know, he's known for writing travel books from different countries. He informed me that he was in the area, so I invited him to dinner," said John.

"Ah, if it isn't Kurt Hammer. I attended journalism in Bodø while you were studying at the Police Academy," said Karl.

"Really, I didn't notice," said Kurt and nodded in Karl's direction.

Jarle immediately got up and walked over to say hello. "Jarle Sørdalen. An honor to meet you," he said.

"Karl Homme, charmed," said Karl.

"I have tons of hotels over all of Norway. Just call me if you need a place to write," said Jarle.

Anastasia sighed. "Jarle, come and sit."

"This is my wife, Anastasia," he said, gesturing toward her.

Karl Homme immediately walked over to Anastasia and kissed her hand.

"Enchanté!" Nice to meet you!

She grinned.

"Jarle, Mr. Homme has a lot to teach you," she said.

Jarle snorted, and his eyes gleamed with hatred, as if he wanted to attack, but Kurt couldn't decide if it was directed toward Karl or Anastasia.

"There, there," John exclaimed. "If everyone would sit down..." He showed Karl to an available seat by Anastasia "...Kurt can tell us the fascinating story about how he ended up here," said John.

Kurt sighed. He carefully extracted a pack of Marlboro Golds from his breast pocket. Looking at Jarle and Karl, he took out a lighter from the same pocket before grabbing a cigarette from the pack. Then he lit it and drew a deep breath.

2

JULY 10, 2014

Kurt Hammer sat in a dark leather chair in a little office in Klostergata 48, Trondheim.

"So, you haven't been drinking for two months?"

The man talking was tall with gray curly hair and a big stomach. The voice had a bass ring to it, which made Kurt ponder whether or not the man had used steroids in his youth.

"No, I haven't," said Kurt.

"Congratulations," said the man.

"I can't sleep, though," said Kurt.

"Why not?" asked the man.

"Guilt. Everyone I shot. Lise and the child," explained Kurt.

"It's been almost two years, Kurt. How long has it been like this?" asked the man. The big man leaned a little forward in his leather chair, but not so far that Kurt felt threatened.

"About a month. I think it started after I'd been with you the last time. 'Started' isn't really the right word. It's more that it started anew. It comes and goes in waves," Kurt answered truthfully.

"Do you think something could have triggered it?" asked the man.

"I don't know. But I don't have anything to do. I miss work," said Kurt.

The big man leaned back and sighed.

"We've talked about this. You are in a vulnerable phase now. If you start working now …"

"… I'll start drinking again. I know. You're the therapist here. Do you have any suggestions?" asked Kurt.

The therapist scratched his beard. "What do you like to do? Do you have a hobby?" he asked.

Kurt put his hands behind his head. "I liked traveling when I was younger, and I like to read," he answered.

"Then I suggest that you take out two extra months of sick leave, travel far away and pack books," said the therapist.

"Really?" asked Kurt.

"It'll be good challenge for you. There's a lot of cheap alcohol abroad, you know," said the therapist.

Kurt smiled nervously. "Yeah, well, challenge accepted," he said.

———

Kurt Hammer sat in a brown leather chair at Starbucks in Kongens Gate in Trondheim. The American jazz singer Melody Gardot's song *"The Rain"* was playing on the speakers, the smell of freshly brunt coffee from all over the world hanging in the air.

She came up from behind, but he still knew she was coming. Her perfume, Chanel No. 5, followed her like a distraught puppy—both in front of and behind her at the same time.

"Hi," she said.

Her candy-apple red lips spread to form a little smile.

"Hi, dear," he said. He turned and looked into her icy blue eyes.

She sat across from him, removed her black leather jacket and hung it on her chair.

"Felicia ..." he began. He didn't come any further, his voice frozen.

She raised an eyebrow.

"... we can't move in together right now. I have to take a couple of months of sick leave and travel," said Kurt.

Silence.

"Really? Why?" asked Felicia.

"Recommendation from my therapist. It's important that I don't start drinking again," answered Kurt.

She sighed.

"I haven't seen you for two months, Kurt! As far as I'm concerned, you might as well travel to the other end of the world. Don't expect that I'll wait for you," said Felicia.

Kurt sighed. "I thought you understood that I had to focus on myself."

"I did! But three months is a long time, Kurt, and I ..." She looked down at the table in front of her "I had been looking forward to seeing you every day."

Kurt sighed. "I understand. But I'm not ready yet," he said.

"Ok. When you come home, I'll be either ready to move in or have moved on, just so you know," said Felicia.

Kurt got up to walk away but kissed her on the cheek before running out into the pouring rain outside.

When he came home to Volveveien 12A, he called his colleague and friend Frank Hansen.

"Frank, do you remember you said I should go to the Bahamas?"

"Yeah, I do, but aren't you going to work soon?" asked Frank.

"My therapist said that I should leave for a couple of months. Do you still think the Bahamas is a good place?"

Silence.

"Hmm, I recently read that traveling to Peru is cheaper than it used to be. Lima is supposed to have a fairly good climate," said Frank.

"Thanks, Frank. I'll check it out."

Kurt took his iPhone away from his ear and hung up with a satisfied smile.

3

JULY 20, 2014

"You've shot many men?"

Anastasia's face had turned white.

"It made the front page of all the biggest newspapers. But you are ... Belarusian, aren't you? Anyway, they killed my wife and child. I was out of my mind. I lost my job for the NCIS but wasn't sentenced for murder, amongst other things, because they were preparing for the largest delivery of cocaine in Norwegian history, but I should obviously have called for backup. Fortunately, I got a job as a journalist after that ordeal."

"You did the right thing," said Jarle. "Without you we might have had a generation of cocaine-addicted teenagers."

"Thanks," said Kurt and smiled apologetically.

"Thanks, Kurt, for that gripping story. Now, my friends, while we're waiting for the food, I'll show you the reason why I invited you here today," John added.

John was never great at being away from the center of attention for more than five seconds, Kurt thought to himself.

John pushed a button under the table. Slowly but

surely, a video screen materialized, sliding down from the roof of the restaurant.

He turned himself and his chair toward the screen when it was all the way down and picked up his cell phone, a Samsung Galaxy Beam i8530.

"Kurt, Rebecca, turn around. You won't want to miss this!"

Both turned as John put the cell phone on the table and started a built-in projector.

"What's that?"

A grayish palette materialized on the screen.

"This, my friends, is a fire-, bullet-, and bomb-proof room in my house. Right now, it contains only the two paintings I've recently procured: *Autumn in Bavaria* and *Several Circles*."

John pushed on the cell phone's screen, and Kurt noticed that when he did it, the camera in the room started moving. Soon it had zoomed in on a painting closely resembling something like an alley surrounded by trees. Then it led to something which looked like a church's spire far away.

"Oh my God!" Jarle exclaimed. "How much did this cost you again?"

"Two hundred and six million. But you already know that ..."

Jarle sighed. "I still can't believe you got *Autumn in Bavaria* that cheap ..."

Kurt turned toward Jarle. "Don't you read newspapers? Aftenbladet just wrote an article about the fact that the price was a record high."

John smiled. "I wasn't exactly portrayed nicely in that story ..."

Jarle snorted. "I could have paid twice that if I wasn't busy that weekend."

"There, there," Anastasia said and patted Jarle on his back. "You can do it next time."

Hugo Friis came out of the restaurant with two deep bowls in his hands.

"First dish," he announced. "Norwegian fish soup!"

All eyes around the table turned toward him as he placed the soup before Kurt and John.

"Bon appétit," he said.

"Looks heavenly," said Rebecca.

When everyone had eaten the fish soup, John turned and directed everyone's attention toward the screen again.

"As you're all probably aware, I also bought another painting, specifically *Several Circles*." Again he engaged his cell phone, and soon another painting showed up on the screen.

Rebecca gasped. "It's beautiful!"

The painting depicted several circles in different sizes on a matte background.

"It is even more beautiful in reality. It reminds me of space," answered John.

"Didn't Kandinsky say that it was his favorite painting?" Anastasia wondered.

Jarle nodded eagerly. "That's correct, dear. He never managed to surpass it later in life."

"So," said Karl Homme, glancing at John with a clever smile on his lips, "a little bird told me that you bought Casa de Aliaga from the Aliaga family and you live there now?"

John gave Karl Homme a stunned glance. "How did you know?"

"I have my sources. It is fairly sad for Lima's many tourists, but good for me." Karl grinned. "You see, I had thought of dedicating a chapter in my new book to it. Now the book will be even more popular. I can visit, John?"

John sighed but smiled a crooked smile. "Of course."

Karl smiled. "Thanks! Is the sword still in the house, John?"

John smirked. "Nothing gets past you, does it? The sword was one of the heirlooms that the family, sadly, insisted on keeping in their possession. Understandably so, considering it is over four hundred years old."

―――――

"Shall we go to the top of the pyramids?" John, satisfied, wiped his mouth with a napkin.

"Sounds like a good idea," Kurt said and put down the teaspoon in his hand.

Tiramisu was normally one of Kurt's favorite desserts, but right now he was so full after eating a double portion of ceviche that a half-finished slice of Tiramisu was left on his plate.

"Agreed," said Karl Homme. "Let's go!" He immediately got up from his chair.

"I'm old and tired and can't be bothered going there. But I can join you around the rest of the area," Rebecca declared.

John smiled. "That's alright. I can pick you up after."

"How fascinating," said Anastasia. "Can you see all of the city?"

"Well, parts of it, at least," said John.

Kurt took a cigarette from his breast pocket and lit it before getting up from the chair and joining the train of people which had begun moving in the direction of the pyramids, led by John Fredly.

"How long did it take to build these?" asked Kurt when they were halfway up the biggest pyramid.

"No one actually knows," John said.

"They offered young women and babies to their god of the sea." John pointed toward a row of skyscrapers in the horizon.

As John came to the top of the pyramid, Anastasia started to scream.

"What is it?" asked Kurt, who still had a few meters remaining before reaching the top.

"Watch out!" Jarle howled as John came backward toward Kurt like a speeding bullet. John held his hands against his throat and landed in Kurt's arms with such speed that the pair of them were about to fall.

Kurt had put down John Fredly and stood over him with a worried look on his face as Jarle and Karl's faces appeared from the top of the pyramid.

"Are you alright down there?" asked Jarle and Karl.

"He's been shot in the chest," said Kurt. "He was dead when he landed on top of me."

4

JULY 20, 2014

Sara Sofia Ulo sat on her double bed in her three-room apartment, sipping a martini and staring intensely at a screen. She had just taken a shower and let her long, black hair hang loose while it dried. The only source of light in the room was her MacBook, which at the moment showed her pictures of dead bodies with entrance and exit wounds. She wrinkled her nose as she scrolled over a particularly gruesome picture of a man who had been shot in the mouth. All that was left of the lower part of his face was a big, red crater. All of a sudden, a new source of light appeared in the room when her cell phone started ringing on top of the nightstand. After a couple of seconds, she peered at it. *Huh*, she thought. *Him? It couldn't be ... Why would he call at this hour of day?*

She grabbed it and answered the call.

"Sara Sofia Ulo, police investigator."

"*Usted no es un investigador the la policía todavía,*" said the deep man's voice on the other end. *You're not a police investigator yet.*

"Because certain people don't give me cases. Today, I

literally had to help a cat down from a tree," said Sara Sofia with badly disguised irritation in her voice.

"Well, right now there isn't anyone else to choose. You have a case. Do you want it?" asked the male voice.

"Now?"

"No, yesterday. Come down to the station immediately."

The man hung up. Sara Sofia looked at her watch, a Rolex Ladies Datejust from 2004. It was a quarter past midnight. *This had better be good,* she thought as she planted her feet on the floor and got up from the bed.

AT THE POLICE STATION, which was a dark glass building on General Vidal Street 250, her boss waited for her in his office on the third floor.

Marco de Sinta, chief of police in the Miraflores district, was a short man with an equally short temper. He had a long face with a couple of grim eyes which blinked frantically when he was angry. He had an aquiline nose which had earned him the nickname *águila*, the eagle.

"What's happened?" asked Sara Sofia eagerly as she came into the office.

"A Norwegian businessman has been murdered. It is a fairly prominent case. It is important that we manage to solve it fast and smoothly. I have put Daniél and Franco in charge of witness interviews because they were available tonight, but they're busy with a different case, so you'll be in charge of finding evidence and solving the case on behalf of the state."

Sara Sofia walked slowly toward Marco's desk. She walked all the way to it, placed both hands at the edge, and leaned in close. She was just a couple of centimeters from his face.

"And have you thought about how I'm supposed to be able to solve the case without witness interviews?"

"What do you mean?" Marco barked.

His small eyes winked with passion. "You will of course be granted the opportunity to listen to the interviews."

"But not ask questions," said Sara Sofia.

"Well, now that you mention it..." Marco pushed Sara Sofia away with his hand. "...I think they need a translator. Can you go down and see to them? They are sitting down in interrogation room five," Marco answered and smiled wryly.

Sara Sofia turned without saying a word and slammed the door shut as she left the office.

5
JULY, 20 2014

A COUPLE OF HOURS AFTER HAVING HELD John Fredly's dead body in his arms, Kurt Hammer sat in a dark glass building on General Vidal Street, more specifically the white interrogation room. Two young police officers wearing black caps pulled down onto their foreheads sat at the other side of a little table, with a microphone in front of them. Because Kurt didn't know much more than tourist-Spanish, the local police had spent an hour finding an officer who knew more than just English from elementary school.

Eventually, they found one, whom Kurt guessed had barely completed the police academy. Now she stood in a corner and translated the ongoing questions, she, too, with a cap pulled down hiding her face. She looked at them with tired, slightly almond-shaped Peruvian eyes.

"What makes you think he was shot, Mr. Hammer?"

"The fact that he has a bullet hole through his chest," said Kurt.

"Then why was he dead when he landed in your arms?"

"Figuring that out isn't up to me. But he held his throat, as I said, when he fell on top of me," said Kurt.

"Okay, Señor Hammer. That's all for now. You may go, but you cannot leave the country before we close this case."

"Hadn't planned on it," said Kurt.

"She can escort you out," said one of the police officers.

Kurt stood up, took out a cigarette from his breast pocket, and put it in his mouth before he walked over to the young lady in the corner. Kurt shook her hand and thanked her.

"Excuse me, you're not allowed to smoke in here, Señor Hammer," said the lady.

Kurt just nodded and walked out the door. As the young police officer, who barely reached his neck, closed the door behind him, he could hear a resigned sigh. Out in the hallway, she lifted her cap. Kurt immediately saw that it was Sara Sofia, but he said nothing.

"Hi, again. I'm lead on this case. I said nothing because no one can know what happened between us! But you should know that you're not removed from my list of suspects," said Sara Sofia.

"John was my friend. I didn't kill him. But I'll be very satisfied if you manage to capture the murderer."

"I ... have to. The number of solved cases here isn't exactly the best." Sara Sofia sighed.

NORWEGIAN BILLIONAIRE KILLED IN LIMA
BY FELICIA ALVDAL AND FRANK HANSEN

The well-known shipping tycoon, John Fredly, was killed tonight, Norwegian time. It is, at present, unclear what the exact cause of death was, though witnesses seem to think he was shot.

Aftenbladet's journalist Kurt Hammer, who at present is on holiday, witnessed the drama.

"He fell from the top of the pyramid and right into my arms. I was about to fall myself but managed to stand on my own two feet. He seemed to be shot in the chest, but I cannot confirm that it is the cause of death," said a clearly shaken Hammer per telephone.

Hammer was invited to the museum and excavation site, Huaca Pucllana, where Fredly organized a dinner party to celebrate his purchase of two paintings by Vasiliy Kandinsky (1866-1944).

The past few years, Fredly has invested vast sums in the excavation work and has said that several decades of excavation work remains.

Deputy CEO of North Sea Shipping A/S, Johan Falk

Michelsen, told Aftenbladet that this is a black day for the company Fredly founded.

"We'll use the next twenty-four hours calming our investors and stockholders. At the same time, this is a black day for me and the rest of the company, and we will therefore grant many of our employees a leave of absence over the next twenty-four hours."

John Fredly was born in Trondheim in 1978 and received his formal education by Norges Handelshøyskole, where he completed a degree in economy and leadership in 2000.

6

JULY 21, 2014

A few hours after Kurt Hammer had gone to bed, his iPhone 5 vibrating on the nightstand by the side of the bed disturbed his attempt at sleeping.

"Kurt! It's Felicia," said the voice on the other end.

Kurt thought it sounded as though she had woken up on the wrong side of the bed and hadn't had time to drink her first cup of coffee.

"Yeah, I heard. Why are you calling? I've had ... a long night," said Kurt.

"I was going to check your mail while you were gone, remember? I went by on the way to work, and you have four unpaid bills totaling 37,500 NOK. One of them has a warning saying the case will go to court if the sum isn't paid in full within two weeks," said Felicia.

"How much is it?" asked Kurt.

"Twelve thousand. Oh my god, Kurt, how could you let your private finances decay like this without letting me know?" asked Felicia.

"I've been sick, Felicia," said Kurt.

"I understand that, but still ... can you fix it? I would

have loved to help you, but I don't have twelve thousand lying around," said Felicia.

"I'll take care of it," Kurt promised.

"You'd better, otherwise you're facing the court in two weeks," said Felicia.

Kurt ended the call and put his head down on his pillow. He had barely closed his eyes before his phone started ringing again. He cursed, opened his eyes, and picked up the phone again.

"Hammer," he answered.

"Hi, Kurt, this is Hugo Friis. Sorry for calling you this early. You're probably just as tired as I am after what happened last night, but I would still appreciate it if you could make it to the old Aliaga house. You know where it is, right?"

"Yeah, I think so," said Kurt.

"Jirón la Union 224. Taking the metro buses is probably the fastest way to get there," said Hugo.

Kurt looked at his Omega Planet Ocean 600m wristwatch, which he had received from Marte when they married. The time was eleven-forty.

"I can be there in a couple of hours," said Kurt.

"Ok, sounds good, but I'd appreciate it if you could be here a little earlier. I have to talk to you."

"I'll see what I can do," said Kurt.

Kurt ended the call and put his head back down on his pillow once more. Then he set an alarm for twelve o'clock. Forty minutes later, he had managed to sleep for twenty minutes and drink a couple of cups of coffee. Then he entered one of the many gray buses, which resembled overgrown wolves, and traveled to and from the Ricardo Palma stop right by the hostel he lived at. Kurt ordinarily hated crowded buses back home in Norway, but taking the bus in

Lima was a different matter altogether. He more or less got the feeling of being locked in a sauna with hundreds of unknown people. He made a mental note telling himself to take a taxi on the way back. At least he had the advantage of being a head taller than everyone he stood next to.

Kurt managed to smoke two cigarettes in quick succession from the moment he walked off at Estación Central Grau until he had made his way to Casa Aliaga.

Casa Aliaga was a wooden house in sixteenth-century Spanish style. It stood out among the buildings in the central part of Lima not just because of its style but because most of the buildings were brick due to the earthquake hazard. The house was painted white with dark brown moldings. The entrance consisted of a brick gate, inside which were two light brown oak doors.

Kurt felt the door handle and realized that the doors were unlocked. He looked around a couple of times before going inside. He walked right into Hugo Friis.

"Oh, excuse me. I didn't see ..."

Hugo smiled broadly. "I was just about to go outside to look for you. Welcome to Casa Aliaga," said Hugo.

Kurt looked around. The inside of the house was covered in champagne-colored bricks, and before them was a staircase leading up to the second floor. An oriental-looking lamp hung from the ceiling. On each side of the staircase stood two black ceramic pots on two porcelain pillars. Plants, probably imported from Spain, grew out of the pots.

"Impressive," said Kurt.

"Well, being a general in Pizarro's day and age was serious business! Let's go to a more appropriate place for a chat," said Hugo.

Hugo led the way for Kurt up the staircase through a

door and into a mustard-yellow room. Its floor was almost entirely covered by a Persian carpet. From the lacquered wood ceiling hung an impressive chandelier with a huge number of candelabras. Hugo sat down in a custom chair of lacquered wood in the middle of the room and signaled to Kurt that he should do the same.

"I don't know if you've realized it, but … police here are corrupt," said Hugo.

"Hmm … I guess I've thought about it," answered Kurt.

"Well, I've made a phone call to John's brother in London, as you do under such sad circumstances, and we both agree that you should take the case! The police will probably close the case unless someone pays them a huge sum of money to do something different. And in any case, they won't do more than absolutely necessary to show that they've investigated it," said Hugo, resigned.

"I'm here, first and foremost, on holiday, to recharge my batteries and make sure I won't relapse," said Kurt.

"Relapse?" asked Hugo.

"I was an alcoholic. I'm in the process of recovering, but I need peace and quiet," said Kurt.

"Is there anything I can do to convince you?" asked Hugo.

Felicia's voice sounded like an echo in the back of Kurt's mind.

The case will go to court unless the sum is paid within two weeks.

"I need 12,000 NOK," he heard himself say.

"So, money, huh? Money isn't an issue. When John's last will and testament is read, I'm convinced that whomever inherits his fortune will help you with money," said Hugo.

Kurt sighed but realized that he might as well continue. "I need it within two weeks," he said.

"Hmm, I see. I can't guarantee anything, but I'll do what I can," said Hugo.

"Ok, I'll take the case," answered Kurt. "But I have a couple of conditions. First, Aftenbladet must get exclusive rights to cover the case in Norway," said Kurt.

"Yeah, and ..."

"I must have the ability to proceed as I want. That includes interviewing everyone present, including you. Understood?" asked Kurt.

Hugo Friis lifted a thin eyebrow and scratched his black hair. "That sounds ... reasonable. I think it should be ok."

Kurt smiled, satisfied. "Very well, let's start with you." He took his cell phone from his pocket and started the recording application then put the phone down on the carved table between them.

"What did you do last night from 18:30 until John was murdered?" Kurt asked.

"At 18:30, I arrived at Huaca Pucllava and went into the restaurant kitchen to check that the cooking had started. Then I started directing the two servers who were present so we would get the china out in time," said Hugo.

"And how long did that take?" asked Kurt.

"We were more or less finished at seven o'clock," said Hugo.

"And where was John during that time?" asked Kurt.

"Here. When I left, he was in his room where he was supposed to change into his dinner suit," answered Hugo.

"Can anyone verify that?" asked Kurt.

"Sure, there are servants and a cook working here. I can take you to meet them later," said Hugo.

"When did John arrive?" asked Kurt.

"Just as we were finishing, he arrived with the widow, Mrs. Swanson," Hugo answered.

"Did they get an aperitif while they waited?" asked Kurt.

"Hmm ... as far as I remember, John had a glass of Chablis Premier Cru, and the widow had a glass of white wine," answered Hugo.

"Can you remember which wine it was?" asked Kurt.

"No, but what does that matter?" asked Hugo.

"Absolutely everything matters," said Kurt.

Hugo sighed. "I can't remember exactly, but I can talk with those who worked in the kitchen."

"Can you take me?" asked Kurt.

"I can probably arrange that," said Hugo.

"One last thing. Is possible that I can get into the safe to see John's paintings?" asked Kurt.

"The safe? Why?"

"Well, the paintings are worth a fair amount of money. It is reasonable to think that they could have been the motive for John's murder. I'm assuming you have access," said Kurt.

"You would be correct about that. But John was very careful to let me know that I shouldn't give the code to anyone but John's heir," said Hugo.

"Did he suspect something was about to happen to him?" asked Kurt.

"In case something happened to John," Hugo tried to clarify.

"But you don't know who the heirs are?" asked Kurt.

"No, unfortunately only the lawyer does," said Hugo.

"And who is the lawyer?" asked Kurt.

"John Christian Elden, of the company Elden DA," answered Hugo.

7

JULY 22, 2014

In Eirik Jarlsgate 6 in Trondheim, the alarm on Frank Hansen's silver-gray iPhone 5s wailed. The time was 05:30, and Frank just managed to stop it from falling down off the nightstand. His wife, Alexandra, looked at him with tired, blue eyes.

"Are you sure that it's a good idea to send her to kindergarten? She's barely two years old," said Alexandra.

Frank yawned and kissed her on the forehead.

"We agreed that it was for the best. I need to work, and you wanted to have a little time for yourself," said Frank.

"Yeah, but then I started to doubt it," said Alexandra.

"It will be okay, dear," said Frank.

Frank was already sitting on the edge of the bed, putting on his Diesel jeans and his white shirt.

When he entered Stine's room, he realized how big she'd grown already.

"Just think, you've already learned to walk," he said loudly to her as he lifted her out of her crib and confirmed a diaper change fortunately wouldn't be necessary before breakfast," said Frank.

He pulled off her nightgown before putting her in a light blue sweater and white pants. Then he took her to the kitchen, where he plopped her down in a black and white BLÅMES children's chair.

Ten minutes later, he took a shower. Thousands of warm droplets penetrated every pore of his skin. When he was done, he still didn't feel awake. In the kitchen, he nearly poured coffee in Stine's baby food. When he finally sat down to feed her, she spat the food in his face.

"Fuck, eat," grumbled Frank.

Stine let out an earsplitting wail and began to cry. Tears started flowing down her small, pink cheeks almost as fast as the raindrops came down over Trondheim.

"What are you doing out there?" Alexandra could be heard saying from the bedroom.

Frank wiped the tears away from Stine's cheeks and kissed her.

"Please eat, dear. Dad doesn't have time for this," said Frank.

He wiped the food away from his face with a napkin resting on the kitchen bench and gave her a tiny spoonful of food, which she, fortunately, consumed. After ten minutes, she had eaten half her bowl.

Frank placed the bowl into the dishwasher before he picked Stine up from her chair and carried her into the outer hallway. There, he put on his black leather jacket before taking down her pink bubble jacket from the peg on the wall. He barely had time to put it on her before they hurried out into the staircase, past the other apartments in Eirik Jarlsgate 6, and out into the rain outside.

Right outside the Nidarosdomen Cathedral, Frank got a phone call from Aftenbladet's editor-in-chief, Harry Karlsen.

"Yeah," said Frank.

"Hi, Frank. Crisis! I'm assuming you're headed for work? There's been a chain collision on the E6 towards Værnes. Can you drive there immediately?" asked Harry.

Frank turned and threw a resigned glance at Stine in the car seat by his side.

"On my way, Boss," said Frank.

Resigned, he hung up and peered at Stine again.

"Looks like you'll have to join Daddy at work," he said and sighed.

He looked in the mirror as he took off toward Munkegaten and made a U-turn. His short brown hair was standing in every direction after he'd been in the shower, but he figured that no one would notice in the rain anyway. His close-set blue eyes blinked a couple of times. He was still tired but thought he could have looked worse, taking the circumstances into consideration.

When he came out of the Værnes Tunnel toward Stjørdal, he realized, to his relief, that the collision had happened on the opposite side of the road. He wouldn't have to walk far. He was greeted by a bloodstained moose squeezed between a silver BMW 2 Series gran coupe and a black Audi coupe. The apparently dead moose had parts of his big and unruly antlers parked in the cars' front windows. Behind the BMW were three cars that had smashed into one another.

Police parked every which way on the sides of the road, in an attempt to avoid further traffic mayhem, didn't make the scene any less chaotic. Frank found a free spot and parked behind a light green police car with its blue lights still running. Then he hurried out of his silver-gray Volkswagen Passat, with Stine still sitting in the front seat. A young, blond policewoman dressed in black beaver-skin pants and a police cap was the first person he noticed. She stood, talking into a walkie-talkie.

"Hi, Frank Hansen – Aftenbladet. Do you know where the person in charge of operations is?" asked Frank.

"He is down there…" She pointed toward a tall man who stood and shouted commands in the rain. "…but I think he is busy. You'll have to go ask him," said the woman.

"Thanks," said Frank.

At that exact moment, he noticed a fire truck coming with its sirens wailing. Frank vaulted back into the car and picked up his Nikon D4S camera before eagerly snapping photos of the firemen in wheat-colored overalls. They jumped out of the fire truck and gathered their electric saws, which they were about to use to free the unhappy persons squeezed inside the cars.

After a couple of minutes, they'd managed to open the roof of the BMW. Frank's stomach twisted when he realized that the people inside were a young couple with a children's car seat in the back. He quietly hoped that the child had died in the stomach of the young brunette. The woman had big gouges in her forehead and a smashed jaw and was probably dead. He didn't want the baby to grow up without parents.

When he had taken pictures of the two being put under blankets, he noticed that his memory card was full. Fortunately, he had an extra in his leather jacket. He hastily switched out the card and snapped a couple of quick photos of the person in charge of operations further ahead. The green and yellow vest that he wore made him look like a tall traffic light in the rain.

When Frank was done, he packed his camera into the military-green camera bag on his back and walked with fast and firm steps toward the person in charge.

"Hi, Frank Hansen - Aftenbladet. Do you have time for some quick questions?" asked Frank.

The tall one turned resolutely and stared at him with two icy blue eyes under a couple of bushy eyebrows. On his head was a black police cap.

"Not really. As you've perhaps seen, a chain collision has occurred because of a confused moose that tried to run across the road. The two in the first car died instantly, and the others are heading for St. Olavs in an ambulance now. They have serious injuries to the head region, and it's uncertain whether they'll live. We're in the process of getting an overview of the situation in regards to the other vehicles. That's really all I have time to say," said the man in charge.

"Thanks," answered Frank. "Your name?"

"Roar Sletten, Trondheim police station."

Frank briefly shook his hand before Sletten turned around. On the way back to the car, he saw, to his relief, that Stine had fallen asleep in the backseat. He worked himself into a trance writing a quick story on his laptop and choosing the most dramatic picture he could reasonably use. It depicted the silver BMW surrounded by firemen and sparks from the electrical saw in the rain.

Half an hour later, he was awoken from the trance by Stine's heart-wrenching cries. He turned and sighed.

"I guess you're hungry again, huh? I guess I'll have to drive you to kindergarten," said Frank.

He finished the story, clicked "save," and to his pleasure noticed that it showed up on Aftenbladet's website before he started the car and drove toward Stine's kindergarten.

———

"Can you explain to me why I got a fucking phone call from Stine's kindergarten?" asked Alexandra.

A murderous-looking Alexandra was the first thing Frank noticed when he came in through the door in Eirik Jarlsgate. Her blond hair was tied in a knot behind her head. Her neat, dark blond brows were lifted and accentuated her blue eyes, which were illuminated with anger.

Frank ignored her and instead turned his head toward Stine, whom he carried on his back.

"Is Mom angry? We've had a good time in kindergarten, haven't we? And you've been with Dad to work today, haven't you?"

"Oh my god, this isn't working anymore," said Alexandra.

She marched resolutely past Frank, took Stine down from his back, and walked out the door behind him.

Frank sighed, bowed down, and started untying his shoelaces. He had learned long ago that it was impossible to discuss anything with her when she was in such a mood.

Suddenly the door flew open behind him.

"The keys," said Alexandra.

"Huh?" Frank asked indignantly.

"The keys! I'm going to my mom's," said Alexandra.

"Really? And when should I come and pick you up again?" asked Frank.

"You can forget about it this time," said Alexandra.

He threw the keys to her. She picked them up and slammed the door shut.

Outside in the rain, Alexandra unlocked the back door of Frank's Volkswagen Passat. With blazing speed, she threw Stine down in her car seat with a grace and softness only a mother can manage when she's angry. When she had made sure that Stine was secured, she walked to the driver's seat, sat down, leaned across the steering wheel, and let tears stream down her face.

Behind her she could hear that Stine slowly but carefully started crying.

"Oh no, Stine. It isn't your fault," said Alexandra.

She walked out of the car again and took Stine in her arms. She clutched her tightly to her breast and stood in the rain for several minutes til she had stopped crying. When Alexandra had wiped both their tears away, she placed Stine back in her seat before sitting down once more in the driver's seat. Then she headed for Stjørdal.

Why am I this angry? Fuck! Of course I know that his job means a lot to him. I've always known that. But he shouldn't put his job over Stine, thought Alexandra.

For a split second, she peered at Stine to make sure she was alright. She was sleeping, apparently. Before Alexandra could turn her head back toward the road, she felt the car starting to skid. Right by Vikanbukta toward Stjørdal, Alexandra slammed on the brakes. The car did a ninety-degree turn and hit the front of a Ford which was coming in the opposite direction.

A minute later, the driver of the second the car ran across the road and realized to his shock that the Volkswagen Passat he had hit at a speed of 85 kilometers an hour had rolled over on its roof.

"Yeah, hi, is it 113? I was just hit by a gray Volkswagen Passat which has now rolled over on its roof! You have to send an ambulance to the E6 by Vikanbukta immediately," he said.

"Ok, thanks for calling. We'll send an ambulance right away," said the voice in the other end.

"Do you know how many people are hurt?" asked the voice

The man kneeled down and looked inside.

"It seems to be … one woman and one child. They're unconscious," he said.

"Thanks," said the voice.

Fifteen minutes later, a fire truck rolled onto the scene of the accident. Its heartbreaking whining made it across the bay as firemen left the truck at the same time. Each of them placed himself by a corner of Alexandra's metal prison and prepared to cut.

Just as the roof of the Passat had disappeared, two ambulances in a shrieking nuance of green and yellow hurried onto the scene. The rear doors were opened immediately and revealed two EMTs in each. A stretcher rolled out from each ambulance.

The unconscious bodies of Stine and Alexandra were driven posthaste in the heavy rain to St. Olav's Hospital.

COLLISION AT E6
BY FELICIA ALVDAL AND HARRY KARLSEN

Late yesterday afternoon, around 4:30, a silver Volkswagen Passat skidded on E6's wet surface toward Stjørdal and collided with a red Ford Siesta ST. The collision happened right by Vikanbukta.

As far as Aftenbladet is aware, the driver of the silver car is now unconscious at St. Olav's hospital. The car is supposed to have had an infant in its rear seat. The child is not supposed to have suffered life-threatening injuries. The driver of the Ford escaped from the incident only suffering minor traumas and immediately called for an ambulance.

Warning drivers

The collision happened just a few hours after a chain collision on the same road towards E6 caused by a moose that had gotten lost and ended up on the road (see the separate story at Aftenbladet.no)

"Because of the weather and temperature, it can be dangerous to drive on E6, and therefore we urge drivers to show extreme caution," said Roar Sletten by Trondheim Politikammer to Aftenbladet last night.

Right now there is a queue from Stjørdal to Trondheim and in the opposite direction. Sletten confirms that the police are working to open the road again as fast as possible.

So far, Sletten cannot say what the reason for the collision was but urges all drivers to change to winter tires as soon as possible.

"It is still legal to drive with summer tires for almost another month, but the conditions now are such that you simply cannot be careful enough. If you're driving, you have to be careful and make sure that your car is prepped for the weather and driving conditions!"

Happened so fast

The driver of the Ford, Arvid Tellefsen, was not able to say much about what happened.

"It happened so quickly, I didn't have time to register what happened before I realized that my car had skidded around its own axis and had been hit by another car. When I walked out of my car to look around, the silver Volkswagen Passat lay on its roof, fifty meters away from my car."

Tellefsen thinks it is a "miracle" that he got away from the experience unscathed and hopes that the driver of the second car will survive.

"The way I understood it from the doctor in the ambulance, she wasn't dead but unconscious. He said to me that if I hadn't called when I did, she definitely wouldn't have survived."

Tellefsen's car has been badly smashed on the right side of its hood, and he says that he will be using public transport for the foreseeable future.

"I haven't tried starting the car, and I probably won't do it for a while. The fact of the matter is that I'll most likely use public transport for the foreseeable future," he says, clearly affected.

8

JULY 23, 2014

The buzzer in Eirik Jarlsgate 6 suddenly rang, dragging Frank out of his dreams. The first thing that hit him was that Alexandra could have forgotten her key.

He sat down on the side of the bed, rubbed his eyes, and looked at his silver iPhone 5S. It told him that it was barely past six in the morning. "Who the fuck comes knocking without an invitation at this time of day?" he asked even as he dressed in his blue pajamas he had thrown on the floor the previous night.

Two men dressed in dark suits met him at the door. Both had matching black ties, belts, and patent-leather shoes. Dark stains on their shoulders told him that it was still raining outside. Frank thought they reminded him of FBI agents from movies he'd seen at the cinema.

"Hi ..." he said, confused.

"Mr. Hansen?" asked tallest one.

"That's right," confirmed Frank.

"Sorry about the disturbance. We had a neighbor let us in. We are from the police department. Can we come in?" asked the tall one.

"What is it?" asked Frank.

"It would be nice if we could come inside," continued the tall one.

"Yeah, sure," said Frank.

Frank opened the door completely and placed himself against the wall.

"Come in," he said and showed them into the living room.

"Sorry about the mess," said Frank.

Folded clothes next to a pile of unfolded ones were on a black living room table from Ikea. A gray corner sofa from Jysk had coffee stains on it. The carpet on the floor was shaggy, and the gray curtains were drawn.

"That's alright," said the shorter man as they sat down on the sofa.

Frank sat down across from them in a dark Henriksdal-chair from Ikea.

"We are, as we mentioned, from the police department. I'm sorry we didn't come before now. It took a little while to locate you. It's about your wife. She wasn't carrying her liccnse."

Frank gasped.

"That's right! Her handbag is in the hallway," said Frank. "Is she under arrest?"

The men shot each other a quick glance before the tallest one continued.

"Not exactly. Your wife and child are in intensive care at St. Olav's. They were in an accident," he said.

Frank Hansen had run a lot in his lifetime. When he was still in secondary school, he'd been best in class at running sixty meters, despite the fact that physical education never was a subject he'd been particularly interested in. When he got up from the sofa, he was down to the end of the street in about a minute. Three minutes later he stood in St. Olav's hospital's reception area in nothing but his night clothes.

"Where is Alexandra Hansen?" he asked.

A blond lady in her forties with big breasts and somewhat protruding front teeth looked up at him with a compassionate gaze.

"Are you her husband?" asked the lady.

"For fuck's sake, yes. Where is she?" he asked.

"She is unfortunately in closed intensive care. Her condition is too critical for you to be able to visit her. She's badly wounded and in a coma. The same thing is true of your daughter, I'm afraid, but her condition is a little more stable, so you can probably visit her in a couple of days," said the lady.

In Aftenbladet's offices on the other side of Trondheim, Felicia Alvdal tried calling Frank.

"Fuck it. Just pick up the bloody phone," she said.

Felicia Alvdal's shapely lips were quivering with frustration.

"He's usually at work before me, and now he's not picking up even though I've been calling for half an hour," she thought as she stormed out of her office.

She was one of the few coworkers at Aftenbladet's new office space in Ferjemannsveien, who had her own office while most did the best they could with partition walls. She hurled through the open office space to editor-in-chief, Harry Karlsen.

"Come in," a voice thundered from inside the biggest office in the building.

Felicia opened the door and lay her eyes at a 150-kilo

man with a shaved head. He sat with his legs propped up on the enormous desk in dark wood, leaning against the glass wall behind him. He'd opened a discreet window to let out the smoke from the cigar in his mouth.

Felicia threw him a disapproving look.

"I know, I know. The wife wants me to quit. I'm trying. Was there anything in particular you wanted?" asked Harry.

"Frank isn't picking up his phone. He's not at work," said Felicia.

She looked at her wristwatch, which displayed 09:45.

"He's probably shattered, unfortunately. Is it ok if I go look for him?" asked Felicia.

Harry nodded approvingly. "Good idea. I approve of your initiative," said Harry.

"Thanks, Boss," said Felicia.

On her way out to the car, she produced her mobile phone and called Kurt.

"Hi, Kurt," said Felicia.

"Hi, dear. What's up?" asked Kurt.

"It ... is complicated. I need to know where you would have gone if you were Frank and needed a drink," said Felicia.

"To drink? Felicia?"

"I KNOW that you don't drink anymore! That's not the point! Where would you have gone?" asked Felicia.

Quiet filled the line for several seconds.

"Try Cafe Dublin, Kongens Gate 15," said Kurt.

"Thanks, Kurt! I'll talk to you later," said Felicia.

Felicia shot through Trondheim's wet and damp streets in her white Mini Cooper S 2002 model. Six minutes later she stood outside Cafe Dublin's black façade. The golden letters over the door glittered in the rain as she walked in.

Inside it was almost completely empty with just a

couple of men in their forties speaking in English with each other.

Felicia walked straight to the bar and asked a blond woman in her mid-twenties with blond hair if anyone had been around lately.

"He is thirty-two years old, has short brown hair, and two close-set blue eyes. His name is Frank Hansen, and he works for Aftenbladet. A slight pot belly," added Felicia.

"Unfortunately, no," said the woman.

"Ok, thanks anyway," said Felicia.

Felicia produced her black iPhone 5 and called Kurt again.

"Olav's Pub? In Olav Trygvassons gate 5? Ok, thanks," said Felicia.

Olav's Pub was in the same building as the Best Western Nova hotel. It was a big, glass building which was situated a stone's throw from the Nidaros Cathedral. Felicia imagined that it had Trondheim's largest outdoor area, but there was no one there at this time of day.

Frank Hansen sat alone by the bar inside the venue. Its interior was dominated by dark wood. Behind the bar, columns in dark wood rose up, concluding in tall spires laden with colored glass. The glass represented roses and a compass, clearly inspired by the pilgrims venturing to the Nidaros Cathedral.

He had three empty beer glasses in front of him, and in his hand he held a half-full Dahls half-liter glass.

"Three Dahls," said Felicia to the bartender.

"Felicia? What are you doing here?" asked Frank.

Frank looked at her with big eyes.

"I'm staying for as long as you are. You needn't say anything, but I can listen if you want to," said Felicia.

Frank nodded approvingly.

"I owe Kurt an apology," he said, his voice cracking.

"How so?" asked Felicia.

"I used to blame him for his drinking ... now I know how he feels," said Frank.

"You're not allowed to say stuff like that," said Felicia. "Kurt has more or less quit, but you'll never get to where he was. You're stronger than that."

Frank snorted and took a big sip from his beer.

"You don't know me well enough to say that," said Frank.

"I know you better than you realize," said Felicia and took a swig of her first pint of beer.

Frank laughed loudly. "Let's hope you're right and I'm wrong. Cheers for self-insight!"

"Cheers," said Felicia.

Five hours later, the pair stood outside Felicia's apartment in Fjordgata in Trondheim. Frank thought that the big apartment complex with beige décor and dark green windowsills reminded him of a small piece of Rome.

"Thanks for following me home," said Felicia.

She kissed Frank on the cheek.

"It was the least I could do," he said.

"Do you live far away? Should I call a taxi?" Felicia asked.

"It's alright. I can call a taxi on my own," Frank said.

Felicia smiled. "You don't want to join me for a glass of wine first?"

She looked at him longingly before leaning in and kissing him.

Frank let her do it for a short while before he pulled back.

"Felicia, I ..." Frank began.

She turned red. "Sorry, Frank, I ... it's been difficult with

Kurt lately. I want him, but he's been completely out of it or not present, and then he all of a sudden leaves for Lima," said Felicia.

"I know," said Frank. "I've ... it's been difficult between me and Alexandra too, but this is just extremely bad timing. I cannot do this right now. Besides, I can't let down ... you have to clear things up with Kurt first. Sorry."

Felicia kissed him on the cheek. "My bad, sorry. Good night and get well soon!"

9

JULY 24, 2014

Early next morning Frank was awoken from his drunken slumber. The ringtone on his phone sounded like an aircraft bombing alert, even from the pocket of his pants. He woke suddenly and looked around. There was no one in the bedroom. When he remembered last night, he let out a long sigh and searched for the cell phone half asleep.

"Yeah, Kurt," said Frank.

"Frank, are you okay? Felicia called and told me what happened," said Kurt.

"No, I'm doing fucking horribly to be perfectly honest. Felicia found me out yesterday, so we drank more than I have for as long as I can remember. At the hospital yesterday, they said that Stine may return from intensive care soon, so I'm really expecting a call," said Frank.

"Oh, I hope they'll be okay. You don't want a vacation, then?" asked Kurt.

"Huh?" asked Frank.

"Well, I just stumbled upon a case down here. I've been tasked with solving the murder of my old friend, John Fredly, and could use your help," said Kurt.

Frank took a deep breath and exhaled slowly. As he let the air out of his lungs, it felt as though every bone in his body was about to break from the weight of what he had gone through.

"You're probably right, Kurt. You're completely ruthless, but you're right. I really could use a vacation. But I don't know if I can leave them now. I ... I just can't do it now," said Frank.

"I don't know if I'd call it ruthless. What's the point in you being there when they wake if you don't have the strength to look after them?" said Kurt.

"You have a point, Kurt. I shall think about it and call you," said Frank.

He dragged himself out of bed. He managed to stand up, but when he was about to move his feet, they were heavy as lead. He almost fell several times, but eventually managed to get to the kitchen.

Half an hour later, he'd made scrambled eggs and bacon, accompanied by a glass of milk. He ate in silence at the kitchen table.

His cell phone was in front of him. He stared at it as though bewitched. Eventually, he gathered courage, picked the phone up from the table, and dialed Grete, Alexandra's mother.

"Yeah, Grete Allstad," she said.

"Hi, Frank here. Are you aware of what's happened?" asked Frank.

"Yeah, I was at the hospital yesterday. They said that I couldn't visit them because they were in intensive care. What about you?" she asked.

"I got the same message, unfortunately. I was out with Felicia from my work yesterday. She ... picked up the pieces that are left of me. Are you going to be at the hospital in the coming days?" asked Frank.

"Yeah, as soon as I get the all-clear, I'll stay there all the time," answered Grete.

"Hmm. A colleague of mine called and suggested that I come down to Lima to help him with a case. I don't know if I'll go, but he suggested that it was best for Alex and Stine if I'm rested and ready to take care of them when they wake," said Frank.

"Lima? Isn't that in South America?" asked Grete.

"Yeah, but I can be back on a plane with a day's notice. Work will pay for it," said Frank.

"Hmm, maybe your colleague is right. I'll be there anyway when they wake up," said Grete.

"Thanks, Grete," said Frank.

When he hung up, he called Harry Karlsen, the editor of Aftenbladet.

"Hi, Harry," said Frank.

"Frank! How are you?" asked Harry.

"I want to throw up," said Frank.

"Are you sick?" asked Harry.

"Yeah, both psychologically and physically, really. I'd thought of calling in sick, but Kurt called ..." said Frank.

"Yeah?"

"He made me realize that I need to charge my batteries until Alexandra and Stine wake up. He said he needed help with a case in Lima, so if you don't have immediate need for me in Trondheim, I'm going to board the first plane to Amsterdam and head south from there," said Frank.

"That sounds like a good idea, actually. Kurt hasn't exactly kept me up to date on what he's up to, but if he needs your help, he's definitely on the trail of a good case. It probably has something to do with the Norwegian who just passed away," said Harry.

"Yeah, Kurt mentioned it. He's going to solve the murder case. We can probably get at least one front-page story out of it," said Frank.

"Just order the tickets on the business credit card and keep me up to date on the development of the case, ok?"

"Ok, that sounds like a deal. I'll call you as soon as I know anything more," said Frank.

"Ok, good luck," said Harry.

"Thanks," said Frank.

A couple of hours later, Frank checked in at the Værnes airport for his flight to Amsterdam. On his way through security, he almost threw up twice, remembering how fervently he hated flying to and from this airport. Weather and wind conditions had not been kept in mind when selecting the location of the airport, which was on a plot of land that had been a farm until 1887. It was more common than not to experience turbulence during landings as well as takeoffs.

Oh my god, he thought when he walked aboard the Boeing 787 plane painted in Norwegian colors. The sound of two Rolls Royce Trent 1000 engines roared despite the constant downpour. *Soon I'll be on my way to the other end of the world. I hope I can manage to be back before Alex and Stine wake up.*

10

FEBRUARY 2, 2014

"What is it?"

Hugo Friis stood in John Fredly's office and looked at his boss with a questioning expression.

John smiled. His dark blue eyes shone with self-confidence. Each and every centimeter of wall surface was covered with book shelves and made the office look small. Hugo always felt trapped in there.

"I'd just like to inform you that I've made some changes to my will. I'm almost forty years old, and after I moved here, I realized that there are things from my earlier life I regret," said John.

"Like what?" asked Hugo.

"Like the fact that I haven't included the people who are nearest and dearest to me in my life in my will," answered John.

"Okay," said Hugo.

"Don't look at me that way! You're, of course, still among them, and therefore you'll be inheriting this house," said John.

"Thanks a lot. Was that all?" asked Hugo.

"Yeah, that was it. Oh, by the way, I need a maid," said John.

"An excellent idea! I'll take care of it right away," said Hugo.

He bowed and left the room.

January 28, 2013

IN THE COURTYARD of the Santa Monica de Chorillos prison, outside Lima, the feeling in the air was electric. The one usually viewed as the toughest of the inmates, "El Muchacho," *The Boy*, had just called another inmate gay. The inmates smelled blood and hovered around the two like a pack of wild wolves. The Boy weighed 120 kilos, was around 1.68 meters tall, and spent most of his time inside the prison working out. Rumors went around that he had steroids smuggled inside.

The man who just had been called gay was 1.8 meters tall and only weighed 88 kilos. He didn't have an extra gram of fat on his body. He had refused to give *The Boy* a cigarette.

Without warning, a punch from the left landed right on his face. It came from underneath, and he wasn't prepared at all. The Boy's massive fist hit right on his nose bone, and the man fell hard on the ground.

The Boy snorted as screams and shouts came from hundreds of other inmates, who now formed a close ring around the two. He bent down to pick up the pack of cigarettes. All of a sudden, The Boy grimaced. A couple of seconds later, he lost his balance and fell over the thin man.

The crowd of people held their breath as the lifeless body of The Boy was slowly eased to one side. The thin man had drawn a knife. As he got up, he was immediately trapped in the iron grip of two big prison guards, who had plowed their way through the throng of people.

January 28, 2014

THE MAN with the broken nose drew in a breath and held it for a few seconds before letting it out and knocking on the door in front of him. The sweat which usually gathered on his forehead, due to Lima's climate, had already had time to gush like a waterfall.

"Come in," said a voice from inside.

The man opened the door, walked in, and bowed.

The person who had answered furrowed his brows and looked up from behind a pair of black designer glasses. His black curls were slightly disheveled on his head, which they had a tendency to do when he was stressed, nervous, or curious—like they were charged with static electricity.

"What is it?" asked John Fredly, straightening his glasses.

"I talked with a buddy of mine the other day," said the man.

"Yeah," said John.

The man coughed. "He works at the restaurant here in the city. It's not even a particularly good restaurant. He earns much more than me per month."

"And?" asked John.

"I wondered if I could get a slight raise? Just a few hundred soles more per month would help a lot. I ..."

"You what?" asked John.

"Met someone. We've talked about moving in together," said the man.

"You're not worth it. With your criminal record, you can be glad that you get the salary you get from me. You're more than welcome to resign, but there won't be anyone willing to hire you," answered John.

The man didn't answer. Slowly but surely, almost unnoticeably, his lips drew into a smile.

"Thanks for your time. I won't bother you again," he said.

The man turned and walked out the door.

11

JULY 26, 2014

When Frank Hansen entered Jorge Chávez International Airport almost two days after his departure, he was extremely tired and really just wanted to sleep. He was about to fall asleep in the passport queue but fortunately managed to stay awake just long enough to get through it. Kurt had promised to show him his hostel, but Frank suspected that Kurt planned to work a little first.

The driver hired to take him to Casa Aliaga to meet Kurt was delayed because of traffic. Frank managed to find the Sumaq VIP lounge, a place with brown walls, gray carpet flooring, and brown Chesterfield chairs. The bartender, a tall, tanned, and overeager surfer type, who sounded like he came from California, recommended the Pisco Sour. Apparently it was Peru's national drink.

Frank sat down in one of the brown Chesterfield chairs and regretted not ordering a beer. Still, there was something about this Pisco Sour, the bittersweet taste, which caressed his taste buds and reminded him of sea and fishing trips with his dad during his youth.

"Hi!"

All of a sudden, a moderately tall man, bald and perfectly dressed in a suit and driver's hat, held up a sign with his name on it outside the lounge.

"Frank Hansen?" asked the man.

"That's right," said Frank.

"Good. I'm supposed to take you to Kurt Hammer. Have you heard about Casa Aliaga?" asked the man.

"No, should I have?" asked Frank.

"You can experience it as we drive," said the man.

The man took him to the longest car Frank had ever seen in his life: a Mercedes Maybach Pullman. He thought it resembled an overgrown family car with its short rear end and round frame. Every part of the car was polished, including the tires. The windows were black, and the car made all the surrounding ones seem like toys. *What has Kurt gotten me involved in now?* thought Frank when he went inside.

The drive to the center of the city took almost an hour and a half. They were motionless several times because of the traffic.

"Is there always this much traffic here?" asked Frank.

"Oh, you're lucky. During rush hour the traffic is much worse," said the driver, looking at Frank and smiling.

When Frank arrived at Casa Aliaga, he took out his cell phone and called Kurt. He looked up at the ancient building with lots of elegant windows and thought, *How did you manage to end up here, Kurt?*

A couple of minutes later, Kurt came out and gave his friend and colleague a big hug.

"Great to see you, Frank. I really hope they'll be ok," said Kurt.

Frank sighed. "I hope so too. I didn't come here to talk

about them. You're not doing too great, yourself ... condolences."

"Thanks," answered Kurt. "It's sad, I'll admit, but working the case helps. Let's go in," said Kurt.

"I don't know," said Frank.

"What do you mean?" asked Kurt.

"You know who owned this house?" asked Frank.

"Francisco Pizarro's best buddy," said Kurt.

"One of the biggest and greediest assholes in the history of the world. Yeah. I researched the house's story on the way here. Casa Aliaga is the former house of General Jerónimo Aliaga, bequeathed by Pizarro, so that they could be neighbors. Aliaga was Pizarro's most trusted general. He was present at the murder of Atahualpa, the last Incan king," said Frank.

"Hmm, that's right. I heard something about a sword during the dinner," said Kurt thoughtfully.

"Oh my god, is the sword still in there? The sword used to murder Atahualpa?" asked Frank.

"No, the family took it with them when they moved out. If you think something will happen to you when you go in there, you've probably spent too much time watching *Pirates of the Caribbean*," said Kurt, laughing.

Frank snorted but reluctantly followed when Kurt showed the way into the house.

Right inside the outer doors, they were met by Hugo Friis. He had short, dark hair and square glasses that framed his round face. He was one hundred and seventy-two centimeters tall and had blue eyes with thin brows. He was dressed in a dark Armani suit.

"Frank Hansen?" he asked with an outstretched hand.

"That's me," answered Frank. "And you are?"

"Hugo Friis. Kurt has told me a lot about you," said Hugo.

"Ah, so he has, huh?" asked Frank.

"Yeah, exclusively positive. I think you'll make a great team." Hugo smiled.

"We will," Frank assured him.

"Well, well. Let me take you up to the second floor. Kurt really wanted to interview the maid, Alessandra Chavez," said Hugo.

Hugo showed the way up a grand staircase, which led to the second floor.

"By the way," said Hugo, stopping in the middle of the staircase. "An episode occurred the night before John died."

"Really? Tell me," said Kurt.

"I guess it happened around three or thereabouts. I was woken up by noises from John's room," said Hugo.

Hugo stopped up, as if thinking about the sounds he had heard.

"Go on," Kurt urged.

"At first I thought maybe it was John, who had woken himself up, but after a minute I felt that I had to go check. I walked down into the hall and went into his room, but John was still sleeping! Then I walked back to my own room and went to sleep again. Today, I checked the room thoroughly. I must have spent at least an hour in there, I think. I couldn't find anything missing. The only one with a key to that room besides myself is Alessandra. Maybe you should confront her with the details," said Hugo.

"Hmm, I'll consider it. Thanks for the information," said Kurt.

Upstairs in the kitchen sat a young woman with blond curls. She couldn't possibly be more than twenty years old. She had big, probing blue eyes and lips the color of aged red wine. She was dressed in a formfitting blue dress which went to her knees.

The kitchen had cream-colored walls and brown leather interior. The furniture had intricate carvings consisting of small men with bulging eyes and gaping mouths, which seemed like they could have been made by Incan slaves. The thought that this furniture was probably touched by Francisco Pizarro made Frank shiver.

Kurt took her hand and presented himself.

"Alessandra Chavez, maid," she said.

She got up and curtsied. Frank took her hand and introduced himself.

"My pleasure," answered Alessandra.

When they sat down, Kurt started the interview.

"How long have you been working for John Fredly?" asked Kurt.

"Oh, not more than half a year," answered Alessandra.

"Do you know if he had any enemies?" asked Kurt.

"It wouldn't surprise me if he did. Business is a dangerous profession. But I never noticed that he did," Alessandra answered.

"What was your impression of him as a person?" Kurt asked.

"A strong person who worked a lot. By the way, I could imagine him having enemies amongst the people working for him, as he made us all work very hard. But personally I didn't mind. He held us to the same standard that he held himself," Alessandra said.

"Did you have any relationship with him outside of your professional relationship?" asked Kurt.

"Obviously not," Alessandra said.

"Excuse me, but you're not from here, are you?" asked Kurt.

Frank stared at Kurt in confusion, and Alessandra gave him a disapproving look.

"I am, as a matter of fact. My mother is Peruvian. My dad is ... I never knew him. My mother has always said that he was at sea," said Alessandra.

"So you never knew him?" asked Kurt.

"That's right," answered Alessandra firmly.

"Not even what country he was from?" asked Kurt.

Alessandra hesitated.

"Of course. I asked Mom that question many times. But it was obviously troubling her, so after a while I let it be," Alessandra answered.

"How is your relationship with your mom?" asked Kurt.

"As I said, it obviously pained her. Most people's parents have one or more sides to them they do not like, Mr. Hammer. Neither I nor my mother are exceptions. We are both humans," Alessandra answered.

"But this is a fairly important side, wouldn't you agree?" asked Kurt.

"My mother has several sides to her that make up for it. She is a warm and caring human being," Alessandra answered.

Kurt smiled pleasantly.

"Thanks for your time, Alessandra," said Kurt.

"You're welcome, glad I could help," Alessandra answered.

When they were about to get up, Frank said, "By the way, how old is your mother?"

"Forty-three years old," Alessandra said immediately.

"And your father?" asked Frank.

"Around the same age, I should think," answered Alessandra.

"Thanks," said Frank.

Everybody got up, and Hugo insisted on following them to the entrance.

"Before we leave, are there more people we should talk with?" asked Kurt.

"Hmm ... the chef, Federico Ruez, was at work during the dinner. I think he's here today," said Hugo.

"Good! Should we check?" asked Kurt.

"Let's do it. When he's not in the kitchen, he's usually in the herbal garden," said Hugo.

Hugo led them out into the hallway, where he opened a side door which hid a staircase. The staircase led up to the roof. A man on his hands and knees was picking herbs from different beds. He was wearing checkered pants and a white shirt. On his head was a panama hat which looked as though it had been passed down through generations.

"Hi, Federico! Our guests would like to talk a little with you," said Hugo.

When the man got up, Kurt guessed that he was around 1.8 meters tall. He had square glasses above dark eyes and a small, thin moustache. His nose was crooked. Kurt guessed that it had been broken and healed incorrectly.

The man came to them and introduced himself.

"Excuse me for asking, but your nose ..." said Frank.

"What happened?" continued Kurt.

"Work accident," said Federico and smiled meekly.

"Ah ..." said Kurt and tried smiling convincingly.

"What can I help you with?" asked Federico.

"Well, Hugo said that you had worked as a chef during the dinner right before John died. We were wondering if you noticed anything out of the ordinary or could give us any kind of information at all about the circumstances," said Frank.

Federico scratched his neck with long fingers.

"No, I didn't really notice anything out of the ordinary," he said.

"Are you sure?" asked Kurt.

"Hugo told me I should make food for one extra person. I didn't understand why, but he just told me to do it," said Federico.

"Interesting," said Kurt.

"Was that all? I ought to get back to the herbs," said Federico.

He brushed off his arms nervously.

"Can you tell me where you worked before coming here?" asked Kurt.

"Is it important?" asked Federico.

"Just answer the question. We are trying to solve a murder here," said Frank.

"I ..."

Federico lifted his neck and looked up into the air.

"I worked at Central Restaurante," he said.

"Is something wrong?" asked Frank.

"No, quite the opposite! Central Restaurante is one of the best restaurants in Lima! But I was fired," said Federico.

"Why?" asked Kurt.

"Because I overslept. But now I really ought to get back to the herbs," Federico said and got up.

"Maybe you can show us out?" Frank suggested to Hugo.

When they were about to exit, Hugo asked Kurt, "Why didn't you confront Alessandra with the episode that happened in John's room?"

"Well, she didn't do anything illegal, did she?" Kurt smiled.

Hugo had to admit that he was right.

"I'll think about the episode and take it up with her when I've found out more," Kurt promised.

"One more thing. When I was in John's room, I discovered that he had received a lot of letters signed 'A.' They were perfumed and seemed to contain elements of love letters. I think that lately he has received some letters without a sender's address. Nowadays, it is unusual to get letters at all, so I thought you might want to know," Hugo said.

"Thank you for the information! I'll think about it," Kurt said.

"She's lying," said Frank when they were sitting in the limousine, heading back to Pariwana hostel. "Either about the relationship to her dad, mother, or both."

"Agreed. And Federico, too. What is the chance that a chef with a broken nose is fired because he overslept? And how could he have broken his nose in a work-related accident? Now we have to prove it," said Kurt.

"Where do we go now?" asked Frank.

"First to Central Restaurante, Federico's old place of work. Then to Dazzler Hotel. It's somewhat far away, so let's take a taxi," said Kurt.

"Dazzler? Who lives there?" asked Frank.

"The known writer of travel books Karl Homme," said Kurt.

Frank stared at Kurt. "Karl Homme? What's he got to do with this case?" he asked.

"He knew John, apparently. I had no clue that he knew John, but he did," answered Kurt.

"I've read a lot of his books, actually. Meeting him will be exciting," said Frank.

"Just remember that we're there because he's a suspect in a murder case," said Kurt.

"Of course," said Frank.

Right then they were passed by a black checkered taxi which stopped as Kurt stretched out his hand.

Twenty minutes of traffic jam later, the taxi stopped outside Central Restaurante at Av. Pedro de Osma 301 in the Barranco district. The building resembled an old, Spanish colonial building. It was made from marble and stood almost three meters high. A brown door flanked by red marble indicated the entrance.

The chandelier by the entrance consisted of sand-colored squares in different sizes that was suspended from the ceiling. Frank wrinkled his nose, and even though he didn't say anything, Kurt agreed. He could imagine Frank thinking that this place was too garish and imbued with modern art, as if it was made exclusively for New Money. Definitely not a place where he'd go out to eat, neither on his own nor with company.

The walls were painted in a shade of iridescent green, and the place was almost empty.

"Can I help you?" asked a tall, thin waiter with slicked-back hair who seemed to be in his late thirties.

"We're looking for the proprietor," said Kurt.

"The proprietor? He isn't working today, unfortunately. What's the matter?" asked the man with an honestly surprised tone to his voice.

"It concerns a former employee, Federico Ruez."

"Ah. I don't know how much we can say about former employees, but he was ... a problem. An incredibly gifted chef but still a problem," said the waiter and sighed.

"In what way?" asked Kurt.

"Why do you want this information?" asked the waiter.

"I'm investigating a murder. I'm a private eye, hired by the family of the victim," explained Kurt.

"I see. I think the manager is working right now. Do you want me to get her for you?"

"I'd love to speak with her," answered Kurt.

The server nodded and signaled to one of the other servers who walked past that she should take care of the customers.

After a few minutes, a small Peruvian lady in her mid-thirties emerged. She wore stiletto heels, and her hair was arranged in a bun on top of her head. She grabbed Frank's hand.

"Aiko Alvarez. Were you the one who wanted to get a hold of me?" she said, looking up at him.

"No, it was me," Kurt said and stretched out his hand.

The little lady was a little perplexed, glaring at the tall Norwegian, who looked at her with eyes that seemed to see right through her. She quickly gathered her wits and shook Kurt's hand.

"As I understood it, you had some questions regarding Federico Ruez," she said.

"Why was he fired?" asked Kurt.

"It started with him coming in late for work. After a while, it was clear he was high at work, too. He received an offer of temporary leave to go to rehab, but he wasn't willing to receive help. After a while, I had no choice but to fire him," she said.

"I see. Thanks. You have been very helpful," said Kurt.

He turned toward Frank and said, "Next stop: Dazzler Hotel!"

As the taxi stopped outside Dazzler Hotel, Kurt looked out of the window. It seemed ordinary, with light brown skyscrapers connected by a square section at the bottom. At the top was something like guard rails, which seemed to grow seamlessly out of the roof. Frank paid the taxi with the business credit card, and together they walked out onto the street and into the lobby. It was chocolate-colored with white columns lining its walls. All the furniture was either white or gray. The room teemed with life; men and women clad in suits sat speaking in different languages on their cell phones. A young Japanese couple shared a big portion of ceviche in a corner, and a man in a gray shirt and khaki pants was sleeping on a sofa. *Probably a journalist colleague,* thought Kurt with a smile. Spherical containers were placed on the tables, and inside were something similar to miniature disco balls which reflected the light.

Kurt walked to the reception and established that Karl Homme lived on the fifth floor, room 689. When he stood outside the room, he knocked, only to find that nobody answered.

A short phone call later, it turned out that Karl was on the roof, about to take a swim.

The swimming hall on the top floor turned out to be completely empty except for Karl Homme. The floor consisted of dark wooden planks, and Lima's skyscrapers were illuminated by the red sunset. The roof was a single big sheet of glass. Out of the speakers on the walls, Simona Severini declared that she was afraid of "the premier moment." The room smelled faintly of chlorine and reminded Kurt of the bathhouses he used to visit in Russia on summer vacations with his mother's side of the family. It gave him a hint of longing for home, in a weird way. Russia was never home for him, just a place he visited. Still, it was closer to home than Lima.

"Sit down," said Karl.

His long brown hair was secured to the back of his head with a hair tie, and under the water's surface, Kurt could see Karl Homme had a slim and athletic body.

Kurt and Frank sat down in beach chairs made of wood, which were placed along the edge of the pool.

"Who is your partner?" asked Karl right before he ducked his head under water for a few seconds.

"Frank Hansen. I'm a journalist for Aftenbladet. We are doing a story on John Fredly's death, and Kurt figured we should talk to you," said Frank.

"Ah. What can I help you with?" asked Karl.

"What did you do the day John was killed ... that is, before you showed up to the dinner party?" Kurt clarified.

"Hmm ... I landed in Lima the day before, and ... that's right! I remember I read the story in Aftenbladet about John Fredly having bought the paintings. Then I decided to call him up and was invited to dinner that same evening. When I was done with eating breakfast, I walked down to the reception to find a good route for jogging. Then I jogged for a couple of hours before I realized that I didn't have a dinner outfit. So then I went to the city center and got a suit. While I was there, I thought that I should do some work, so I visited the catacombs in Convento, took some pictures, and wrote a chapter for my book," said Karl.

"Then you went home and changed before going to the dinner party?" asked Frank.

"That's right," answered Karl.

Karl had already swum to one end of the pool and was heading back.

"Did you know John Fredly from before?" asked Kurt.

"Not really. He attended the release party for my previous book. He is—was—fond of traveling. I guess it was one of the reasons he ended up here. But if he'd had the opportunity, he'd probably have traveled more," answered Karl.

"What makes you say that?" said Kurt.

"He was a restless sort of person. Most people fond of traveling are, on one or more levels. He obviously had problems here, so he would probably have moved on somewhere else," said Karl.

"Problems? What problems?" asked Kurt.

Karl Homme climbed out of the pool, grabbed a white towel from the floor, and lay it around his neck. He walked over to Kurt and looked him in the eyes.

"He was murdered, wasn't he?" asked Karl rhetorically.

"Are you implying that he was murdered because he had problems?" asked Frank.

"He was a rich man. He was worth several hundred million NOK. Everyone with such a fortune will, at some point in time, be surrounded by people who … would prefer to see them dead," answered Karl.

"Do you have any concrete names?" asked Kurt.

"No, not really. I just remember him saying to me at the party that he didn't feel he could trust the ones he worked with. Maybe the guy was paranoid or maybe he had just lost touch with the real world by having access to too much money. Or maybe he just happened to have had a point. After all, he's dead now," answered Karl.

"Do you think he was murdered by someone in his close circle of friends?" asked Frank.

"Who else could it be?" answered Karl.

12

JULY 20, 2014

A man stood at the top of the pyramid and looked down at John Fredly, who came walking toward him.

John had curly, black hair which lay neatly arranged in a bun on top of his head. He smiled and stopped for a second to enjoy the view. Behind him, at the very bottom, walked the accursed journalist. *How was it possible to spend that much time getting up a pyramid?!* The journalist had been an unforeseen element. But the plan was going to happen, no matter what.

Besides, the bastard had made it personal. *Fuck, I can't believe how much I hate you,* thought the man. A couple of seconds later, John stood in front of him, on his way to take a final step and put his feet on the top.

"If you're not already dead, you'll certainly die now," the man whispered before extracting a small cutlass with a gloved hand, stabbing his target right underneath the heart. It had the desired effect. John's eyes opened slowly in a revelation of fear, understanding what was about to happen. He fell, down, down, down, before finally landing in Kurt Hammer's lap.

THE CURIOUS CASE OF ALESSANDRA CHAVEZ PART 1
JUNE 2005

Alessandra Chavez had never been a normal child. She grew up without a father, and no matter how much she whined, she never managed to extract any real information from her mother. Her dad had apparently gone sailing and never returned. During her childhood, she had quietly accepted this version of the truth. Still, she could see that everyone around her was different. As her mother, Agatha, loved to point out, she was "not stupid."

"Who's your father, Alessandra?" her best friend, Maria Velez, asked one day in the tenth grade.

She and Maria Velez sat on a bench in the schoolyard of Colegio Pestalozzi. Maria looked like a typical Peruvian: light brown skin, chocolate-colored almond-shaped eyes, raven hair, and pearly white teeth. She was a head shorter than Alessandra. On one of her cheeks she had a small mole.

"I can see that you're nothing like your mother. She looks more like me than she does you," said Maria.

Alessandra sighed. "I don't know, Maria. Every time I

ask, I just keep hearing that he's gone sailing. But of course, you're right. I mean, look at me ..." said Alessandra.

Maria looked. By her side was her best friend, and she had light curls, dark blue eyes, and skin that was just a touch lighter. She was a full head taller—and she had been for as long as the pair had known each other.

"What if we go home after school, Alessandra, and look for something? Your mother must have some clues," said Maria.

"Like what?" asked Alessandra.

"I don't know. Something, anything! Anything at all," said Maria.

Alessandra smiled. "I don't know if Mom would like it."

"She can't just keep telling you that he's at sea when he's never returned," said Maria.

"Yeah, well, you're right! Let's do it," said Alessandra.

Alessandra and her mother lived in a rusty red and white apartment with a tin roof above a restaurant. It was painted azure blue and had red and yellow moldings. To get to it, you had to go through the restaurant and out to a staircase in the back. Alessandra never tired of going through the restaurant. New people were always sitting there, and every hour of the day, you could experience interesting conversations, sounds, and smells.

Freshly ground coffee from the farms in Colombia was the smell she liked best, but she also loved the smell of Chef Santiago's tomato soup, the smell of tobacco from Pedro's pipe, and the sound of lovers reciting love poems to each other when she went to bed on the floor above.

"Don't you tire of living above this restaurant?" asked Maria when they were heading up to the apartment. "How do you sleep?"

"I have grown used to the sounds, so now I can't sleep

without them." Alessandra smiled. "So, what are we looking for?" asked Alessandra as they walked into a tiny hallway. It had wooden floors and white walls. A hook shaped like a little lawn gnome hung on one of the walls. Three doors led to a bathroom, a living room, and a little kitchen with a little loft.

"I dunno," said Maria. "But your apartment isn't exactly big, so if there is a clue here, it has to be in a place you haven't thought of."

The two girls hung their clothes on the hanger. Maria was wearing a little black jacket over a T-shirt with the inscription "Fri Yay." Alessandra was wearing a pink bubble jacket over a red dress with white dots and a white belt around her waist.

"I can take the living room if you take the kitchen," said Maria.

"Ok," said Alessandra.

Some forty minutes later, the two girls had looked through the apartment top to bottom. They had even helped each other take apart an old sofa in the living room as much as they could without completely demolishing it.

Now they were sitting in the kitchen, drinking coffee from oversized cups, over a red kitchen table. On one of the walls hung many pictures from Alessandra's childhood. Her mother was in none of the photos, except for one picture where she was sitting on a rooftop, which seemed suspiciously like the roof of the apartment. She stared out towards Lima, her black hair fluttering in the wind. She looked like she couldn't be more than twenty-two.

"Do you know who took that photo?" asked Maria and pointed to it.

"Grandfather, or so my mom told me," said Alessandra.

"Something's not right about it," said Maria.

Alessandra gasped. "You're right! I have never thought about it before," she said.

The picture was sitting somewhat off kilter in its blue frame. It was almost impossible to notice unless you were looking for something that was wrong.

Alessandra put down her cup with shaky hands and slowly got up. She walked across the floor and took the picture down from the wall. Her gilded curls shone like gold in the weak light penetrating the kitchen window.

She turned and looked into Maria's chocolate-colored eyes. Both held their breath as she walked back and put the image on the table.

"Are you going to open it?" whispered Maria.

"I almost don't know if I dare," answered Alessandra.

Maria clutched her hand and held it in an iron grip.

"I'm here for you," she whispered.

Alessandra nodded. She turned the photo and started opening it from the back. Soon, the two friends had helped each other separating the back plate from the frame. With shaking hands, Alessandra took the photo which was located under the plate and turned it.

By her mother's side was a young man in his mid-twenties. He had short, dark hair which stuck out every which way. He was a head taller than Alessandra's mother and skinny. Alessandra thought he looked handsome, but it wasn't easy to tell when his back was facing the camera.

The two friends gasped.

"Do you think ..." asked Maria.

"I ... don't know," answered Alessandra. "But why would she have hidden it if not?"

Right then the outer door opened.

"Alessandra, are you home?" asked a voice.

Alessandra and Maria held their breath.

"Maria, are you here too?" asked the voice.

"Hi, Agatha! Busy day at work?"

Agatha Chavez had just popped her head into the kitchen from the hallway. She looked like a postcard picture of a Peruvian woman: dark hair in two long braids, a fairly triangular face, chocolate-colored, almond-shaped eyes, and pearly white teeth. Her skin was weathered and wrinkly, especially around the eyes and the mouth.

"Oh, always. Many tiresome customers to deal with, you know, the usual ..." she began.

Alessandra got up. She turned toward her mother, looked her in the eyes, and stretched out the arm with the photo.

"Mother, why haven't you told me the truth?" asked Alessandra.

Her mother immediately ran off. When she came back ten minutes later, she was, at first, completely silent. She said nothing and sat down, looking at the photo once more.

"He was my first love. But he was completely open about the fact that what we had couldn't be more than a fling. He was on vacation to celebrate his master's in business, and he didn't exactly have plans to move here. I accepted it and held onto him for as long as I could. Of course, only once he'd left the country, I found out that I was pregnant with you, Alessandra," said Agatha.

"Why didn't you tell me anything?" asked Alessandra.

Alessandra heard her voice grow surprisingly loud, while at the same time she was almost crying.

"I ... was obviously going to tell you, dear. But I had no way of contacting him, so I thought maybe it didn't matter," said Agatha.

"No way," said Alessandra.

"All I have is an old telephone number. When I was

about to call him to tell him I was pregnant, he didn't answer, and I was never able to muster the courage to call him again," said Agatha.

"Do you still have the number?" asked Alessandra.

"Hm ... it's probably in a drawer somewhere. But you can't get to him now. I think it was the number to the student dormitory he lived in in Norway. He told me that he lived and studied all the way up north, in a small town called Bodø. He was from a bigger city further south. Trondheim," said Agatha.

Only now, Maria decided to interrupt. "Was he handsome?" she asked.

"Oh, very," Agatha answered with a smile. "But you can maybe see that in the photo, he actually resembled a Peruvian, with dark eyes and jet-black hair. He had the world's most charming smile and laughter, which could wake people from the dead," said Agatha.

"Haha, Miss Chavez. I think you must have been in love," said Maria.

"As I said, he was my first love." Agatha sighed.

"Do you remember his name?" said Alessandra.

"Of course, dear. John. John Fredly," said Agatha.

Agatha could still remember the first time she had met the charismatic Norwegian at a fishing market. She had walked fast, without looking, and all of a sudden she had walked straight into his chest.

"Perdón," she exclaimed.

She was about to go further, but one way or another her chocolate brown eyes had met his dark ones. He smiled to her as if it was the first time he had smiled at another human being. She couldn't avoid smiling back. She felt it as if she were beaming up at a giant; he stood almost two heads taller than her. He was dressed in a light blue Hawaiian shirt and had a red bandana around his throat.

"Do you know where I can find the best ceviche here?" he said in Spanish with a heavy accent.

Her cheeks immediately grew a little redder than usual.

"Where are you from?" she asked and tucked her long dark hair behind her ear.

"Norway," he answered.

"Whoa, that's far away! You're fond of fish there, aren't you?" she asked.

"For the most part, we eat polar bears which we catch with our own hands, but we like to try local dishes when we are abroad," he said with a clever smile.

She couldn't stop herself from laughing.

"Let me show you. I was on my way to buy dinner anyway," she said.

When the mystical Norwegian had received his pieces of fish in glossy paper, he turned around and beamed at her.

"Now, I'm just missing company for dinner," he said.

"Well ..." She thought about it for a minute. "I'm eating dinner anyway. I usually eat dinner in a park not far from here. You can join me there, if you want," she said.

Soon, they were sitting and watching small children and their parents throwing breadcrumbs to local pigeons while Japanese tourists were photographing everything around them.

"What are you really doing here?" she said.

"I am on vacation. I just finished my master's in business and thought I deserved a little break. This is actually my first time traveling all alone," he said.

"No, are you kidding me?" she asked.

"No, I always used to travel either with my family or friends," he said and laughed.

"And how do you feel about it so far?" she asked.

"Traveling alone? It ... well, I'm meeting the locals, at least. And I've gotten to know people from all over the world. I live at a hostel in the Miraflores district. The money goes further that way, and it is incredibly social," he said.

"And what is your impression of the locals?" she asked.

"Well, some of them are incredibly beautiful. And the food they help me find is ... not as good as the fish in Norway, but still fantastic," he said and smiled.

"Haha, you'd better watch your mouth. I've grown up on this food," she said.

"It's probably even better if you get it prepared by your parents. Was your mother a good chef?" he asked.

"She's worked as a chef all her life, actually. But I probably like the food here better than the customers. Nothing can beat the taste of mom's homemade food," she answered.

"Where are we now?" he asked, looking around.

"We are in one of Lima's largest parks, actually. The park is called Parque de la Exposición. There is a museum, Museo de Arte, here. Would you like to join me there?" she asked.

"Why not? I haven't made plans for the day," he said.

"Let's go," she said and got up.

Many hours later, she sat on the roof of a house built over a restaurant. The sun was about to go down across the rooftops in Lima. Agatha and John held each other's hands.

"Have you lived here for a long time?" asked John.

"We've lived here for a couple of years," answered Agatha.

"It has its charms, but I don't know if I'd ever get used to having to walk through a restaurant every time I wanted to go home," said John.

"Haha, I think it is cozy. I'm on a first name basis with all the staff and the regulars," said Agatha.

"Do you get a discount?" asked John.

"Maybe. But if you want it, you have to keep coming here to keep me company," said Agatha.

"Agatha, I'm just on holiday. I must return to Norway …"

"Don't say anything more," said Agatha.

She leaned in close, embraced him, and kissed him fervently and intensely.

THE STRANGE CASE OF ALESSANDRA CHAVEZ
FEBRUARY 10, 2014

The bridge *Puentede los Suspiros* in Lima's Barranco district was witness to thousands of tourists coming and going across it every year. Maybe they were drawn to it by the same amorous magic which drew José María Eguren, Rafael de la Fuente Benavides, and Julio Ramón Ribeyro to it in their time and was the reason for the name. The water under the bridge had disappeared and made way for a path, which led to the beaches where the ocean met the cliffs in Barranco. Other than that, the bridge was exactly as it was constructed in 1876 to connect the Ayacucho street with a yellow Catholic church, where local fishermen came to pray for mercy and forgiveness. But it wasn't just tourists and infatuated poets finding their way to the Barranco district.

Alessandra Chavez yawned and looked at her watch. It showed 06:50. She jumped out of the bed and walked right into the bathroom. The sharp light stung her eyes.

"Oh, lord," she gasped.

She was having a bad hair day. Her golden curls were a matted mess. It was time to take a shower.

After a refreshing shower, she spent fifteen minutes putting on simple but effective makeup.

In the hallway to the kitchen, she met her roommate, Tricia.

"Oh, Alessandra, you look really professional," said Tricia.

Alessandra smiled. The blunt Southern American probably wouldn't have said it if she didn't mean it.

"Thanks! I have to look good today, you know," answered Alessandra.

"Oh, that's right. You're going to an interview, aren't you?" asked Tricia.

"Yep. Must be there in an hour," answered Alessandra.

"You are lucky! I have never been there before," continued Tricia.

"Should I take pictures?" wondered Alessandra.

"Yeah, why not? A photo or two would be nice," answered Tricia.

"Haha, maybe I can take a photo with my phone. We were going to meet after the lecture today, weren't we?" said Alessandra.

"I guess so. I'm looking forward to hearing all about it," said Tricia.

"I'm really excited," admitted Alessandra.

"I understand that," said Tricia.

"I ... not in that way. Or, that way too, but I'll tell you more later tonight," said Alessandra.

Tricia looked curiously at her roommate with intense, green eyes.

"Like I said, I'll tell you more later tonight. Go to the bathroom now so you won't be late for class," continued Alessandra.

"Ok, Miss Secrecy," said Tricia and continued to the

bathroom.

A little later, Alessandra boarded the metro bus heading toward the center of Lima. She just managed to squeeze in. She took her cell phone up from her bag and called her best friend, Maria Velez.

"Hi, Maria! Guess where I am?" asked Alessandra.

"Are you there already?" asked Maria.

"Haha, no, but I'm on my way there. I'm standing on the metro right now," answered Alessandra.

"Haha, just as full as always?" asked Maria.

"You'd better believe it! I just managed to squeeze in," said Alessandra.

"I don't doubt it. I don't exactly miss it, but things aren't much better here in London. I'm lucky if I get a seat half of the time," said Maria.

"How are you doing over there?" asked Alessandra.

"Oh, Alessandra, I love it! The friends I live with are super nice. They had bought flowers for me and picked me up at the airport," answered Maria.

"Wow, that sounds amazing! I hope you'll do okay at the university."

"Well, medicine isn't known for being an easy subject. But I'm motivated. I hope you are too, even if I don't understand why you don't want to study."

"Well, it'll be a bit strange working for my dad, but ..."

"And you're sure that you'll get the job?"

"If not, I'll just apply somewhere else. I'll talk to him, no matter what."

"And you're sure that it's him?"

"How many Norwegians with that name are here in Peru? There's barely five million of them in the world."

"But you have no evidence?"

"Not except for the picture. But if he refuses to hear me

out, I'll get proof. DNA proof!"

"I wonder if he's as stubborn as you. You certainly didn't get that from your mom. Good luck, anyway."

"Thanks, babe. I must get off the metro now, but I'll call you tonight to hear about your first day of your studies. You must promise to tell me everything!"

"You too! I'll talk to you later!"

When she had squeezed out of the metro bus, she took a deep breath of fresh air. Thirty minutes later, she was in front of Casa Aliaga. The elegant wooden building was, in spite of its relatively unique façade, almost invisible in the center of Lima.

The second floor consisted exclusively of windows. They were oblong and checkered, designed in sixteenth-century, Spanish style. The first floor consisted of a kiosk and a small restaurant, completely unrelated to the two doors leading into the house.

She knocked on one of the two big entrance doors made of wood. The handle formed a lion's head the size of two hands on top of each other.

Almost immediately, the door was opened by an older gentleman, who appeared to be in his late forties. He had short, dark hair and square glasses which framed a round face. He was one hundred and seventy-two centimeters tall and had blue eyes, thin brows, and was immaculately dressed in a dark suit from Armani.

"Hi! My name is Hugo Friis!"

His English accent was difficult to place. *Probably Norwegian,* she thought.

"Alessandra Chavez," she answered, took his hand, and smiled her broadest smile.

"Oh, you're here for the position as a maid?"

"That's right!"

"Ok, please come in! Sorry I haven't had a complete overview. Twenty different people have been here during the day and yesterday for different positions."

"That's alright," she said and walked across the doorstep.

She gasped. She had seen many pictures of the place, but had never been there before the place was bought by John Fredly as so often happens when living in proximity to tourist attractions. She concluded that the pictures really didn't do the place justice.

The inside of the house was covered in champagne-colored bricks, and before them was a staircase leading up to the second floor, situated under an oriental looking lamp which hung from the ceiling. On each side of the staircase stood two black ceramic pots on two porcelain pedestals. Plants probably imported from Spain grew out of the pots.

Hugo Friis followed her up to the second floor and into the kitchen. The kitchen had cream-colored walls and brown wooden furniture. In one corner stood a fridge in brushed metal. Alessandra couldn't decide whether the interior resembled an antiquity or an object from outer space. The furniture had intricate carvings consisting of small men with bulging eyes and gaping mouths, which seemed like they could have been made by Incan slaves.

"First question. Could you imagine yourself living here? I'm aware that you could probably arrive at six every day, but we'd prefer you moving in, as it is technically part of the job description."

"Well, I already live with a flatmate, but ... are you kidding? The place is amazing!"

"I have been Mr. Fredly's butler and personal assistant for close to fifteen years, Miss Chavez! I never joke when it comes to work. But it's good that you like it."

From the kitchen, they walked to one of the two salons

and sat down. The room had a dark wooden floor with an intricate checkered pattern. Two identical red Persian carpets with gold details lay on the floor. On one of the walls hung a portrait of Jerónimo de Aliaga, the first owner of the house. By its side was a portrait of his wife and another of his daughter. On each side of the portraits hung big mirrors with ornate golden frames. On the second wall hung a round mirror, also in a golden frame that was decorated with floral patterns. The ceiling was white, and from it hung a big chandelier suspended from golden chains. Around it, the ceiling was decorated with more intricate golden floral patterns. In each end of the room stood two tables, surrounded by cushioned chairs and sofas.

Hugo indicated that they should sit down at one of the tables. They each sat on a side.

"What kind of experience do you have?" asked Hugo.

"Well, to be completely honest, no work-related experience. But I'm a clean person by nature, and I've been raised by my mother to take the dishes and clean up after every meal," answered Alessandra.

"You're aware that women who have worked in hotels for many years have applied to the position?" asked Hugo.

"I believe you, Mr. Friis, but I'm convinced I can do a good job. I will give it my all, and I'm not studying. What I can't do, I'm sure that I can learn," answered Alessandra.

"Hmm, well, at least you have the right attitude," mumbled Friis, and he fished out a notebook from the inside of his suit. He started taking notes.

"What is your motivation for applying for the position?" asked Hugo.

"I simply want to work. I always got good grades at high school, but I'm tired of both school and studies ... at least for a few years. Mom obviously wants me to start at university, but I've already said that I can't be bothered. So when I discovered this position, which fits my personality so well, I just had to apply!"

Hugo Friis eagerly took notes but kept a poker face.

"Can you make coffee?" Hugo asked.

"Oh yeah. I love coffee! I drink at least two cups a day, myself. Now, I don't know what kind of coffee Mr. Fredly prefers, but whatever it is, I would think I could make it," answered Alessandra.

"Are you willing to do things which aren't included in the job description, such as buy food, make and serve coffee to several persons, and maybe even converse with guests if necessary?" Hugo asked.

"Why not? I see no reason why I shouldn't be able to do it," answered Alessandra.

When Hugo was done making notes, he said, "Thanks, Alessandra! That was it! You'll hear from me."

They got up and shook hands.

When Alessandra was on her way to the metro, she was filled with an enormous sense of disappointment. *How could I be so stupid and say I had no experience? I should have at least pretended to have some,* she thought.

In the evening, Alessandra Chavez lay in her bed in her flat in Lima's Barranco district. The room was little, barely three square meters, but it was light and airy. It had a large window on one end, and she loved that she had found a room in the Barranco district. Every day she walked past couples kissing in front of cameras and feeding doves in the park. She traveled to many markets where all kinds of fresh fruit were being sold, along with swordfish from the harbor in Callao and coffee beans from Colombia. She encountered fishermen on their way to the markets with their catch of the day.

Right now, she dialed Maria in London.

"Hi, you! How was your first day of studies?" asked Alessandra.

"Oh, hi, Alessandra! The first day was stressful. We were shown around the institute, got to meet our mentors, and received information about our lectures for the first semester. Then we spent time getting to know the other students. I got to know a handsome student named Mark. He's from Ireland," said Maria.

"Oh, Maria, how exciting! You must keep me informed. Did you get his number?" Alessandra asked.

"Haha, not yet. But we talked about reading together. I think that could turn out well. And what about you? Did you get the job?" Maria asked.

"He was going to call, but I don't feel certain that I'll get it. I have no experience, and he was wondering about that," answered Alessandra.

"Oh, Alessandra, you'll get it on charm alone. I'm absolutely convinced," said Maria.

"Haha, it's good that at least someone believes in me," answered Alessandra.

"I have my fingers crossed for you," answered Maria.

"Thanks! I think I should get to sleep now. Is it late over there?" asked Alessandra.

"No, the time is almost seven. I'm on my way out of bed," answered Maria.

"Oh, have a good day, babe. I'll call you in the morning," said Alessandra.

"Good night," said Maria.

In Casa Aliaga, John Fredly and Hugo Friis sat in the kitchen, discussing the people who had applied for positions.

"So, the maids ... which one did you think was the best candidate?" John Fredly asked.

"Well, there were several good candidates," Hugo admitted. "Both Patricia Valejo and Maria Sanchez excelled. But Sanchez ..."

"What about Alessandra?" asked John.

"What do you want to know?" asked Hugo.

"Was it her?" asked John.

"Hm ... she didn't look like she was Peruvian," answered Hugo.

"Hire her," answered John.

"Are you sure? She doesn't have any previous experience. She said so herself," said Hugo.

"Are you opposing me?" asked John.

"I'm just giving you my honest opinion," answered Hugo.

"Hire her," said John again.

The next morning, Alessandra was awoken by the telephone, which vibrated on its nightstand.

"Hi, is this Alessandra?" asked a male voice.

"Yeah," answered Alessandra.

"Hugo, here! We would like to hire you," he said.

Alessandra let out a little howl of joy.

"Alessandra? Hello? Are you okay?" asked Hugo.

"Yeah, yeah, I just ... Thank you so much," answered Alessandra.

"Can you be here in an hour?" asked Hugo. "John would like to have coffee before starting work!"

"Yeah, yeah, of course," answered Alessandra eagerly.

Alessandra jumped out of her bed and ran into the bathroom when Hugo had hung up. Twenty minutes later, Maria called her when she was standing on the metro bus on the way to the center of the city.

"Oh, my god, Alessandra! I was just about to go to bed when I received your message. Congratulations," said Maria.

"Thanks so much! What coffee do you think he prefers?" asked Alessandra.

"Coffee? I don't know! I take my coffee black. My dad taught me that," answered Maria.

"I bought half a kilo of beans from Colombia at the market. I think I'll make it black. Maybe it's like an audition," wondered Alessandra.

"Make it black! I'm sure it'll be okay. Good luck," answered Maria.

"Thanks, I'll need it," said Alessandra before she hung up.

In Casa Aliaga, Hugo immediately brought her into the kitchen. Along the wall was an old window with a view of the street outside.

"Here," said Alessandra and took up the bag of beans she had bought at the market.

"Ah, I like that you're well prepared," said Hugo. "Federico Ruez, the chef, is sick today and had to be home. It would be nice if you could make coffee and serve it to John. I have made breakfast, but he'd like to have coffee before starting today's work. He likes it black!"

"Great. Do you have a bean grinder?" asked Alessandra.

"Yeah, it's in the cupboard under there," Hugo said and pointed at one of the worktops under the old window with a view of the street. "Now, if you'll excuse me, I have to go, seeing as I have a few things to take care of."

"Where is John's office?" asked Alessandra.

"Oh, it is right down the hall and to the left," answered Hugo.

"Ok, thanks," said Alessandra.

Fifteen minutes later, she had ground some of the beans she'd bought and placed the rest of them with the grinder in the cupboard. She had made the coffee a little stronger than she normally did but confirmed that it still tasted okay. In one of the cupboards she'd found a serving tray, and in another she'd found a big porcelain cup.

Then she added a couple of croissants which she'd also bought at the market, before she carried everything into the hallway. She hesitated for a moment before she carefully knocked on the door, balancing the tray in one hand. She assumed it had to lead to John's office.

"Come in," said a deep voice from somewhere far inside.

Alessandra sighed and set the serving tray on the floor, as she realized that she couldn't open the door. Then she opened the door and hurriedly picked up the tray.

"Hi," she said a little meekly. "I'm the new maid, Alessandra Chavez!"

In front of her she could see a man with dark curly hair, sitting in an office chair in front of a big desk. The walls of the room were completely covered in book shelves, which were overloaded with books of all sizes and shapes.

The man turned toward her and smiled. He had light brown skin and blue eyes which resembled her own.

"Ah, good to see you! Are you coming with my morning coffee?" asked John.

"Yeah, right from the market in Barranco," answered Alessandra.

"Oh, fantastic," answered John.

Alessandra placed the tray on his desk and immediately grabbed the coffee and a croissant.

"Excuse me, Alessandra, but where are you from? You don't look Peruvian," said John.

"I'm half Peruvian. My mother conceived me with a sailor. He hasn't yet come back," said Alessandra.

"Really? I cannot imagine how it would be to have to grow up without a father. It must be horrible," said John.

"I've done alright. But it hasn't always been easy. You're right about that," said Alessandra.

"Do you know you where this sailor came from?" asked John.

"No, mother never told me," said Alessandra.

"She didn't know or didn't want to say?" asked John.

"I guess I asked her a couple of times when I was younger, but she didn't want to say anything about it. It was never brought up after that," said Alessandra.

"I see. Well, your coffee is exquisite. My chef, Federico Ruez, knows many things, but he was never a capable barista," said John.

"Oh, thank you so much," said Alessandra.

"Maybe you can keep on making it?" asked John.

"Oh, yeah, I'd love to," said Alessandra, enthralled.

"Wonderful! But now I unfortunately have to work, and you probably have things you need to do, too," said John.

"Of course. I won't disturb you any longer," said Alessandra.

Alessandra picked up the tray and John's empty cup and left the office.

Outside, after she'd closed the door, she stopped. She looked back.

Should I go inside and say that I'm your daughter? she asked herself.

She could hear her heart beating heavily, and all of a sudden she felt extremely warm and sweaty.

No, it can wait, she thought and continued into the kitchen.

13

JULY 27, 2014

Kurt's iPhone 5, which lay on his nightstand, chimed at 10:30. He looked at it with tired eyes, and it turned out that the caller was unknown. Kurt yawned and pushed the green button on the screen to take the call.

"Hi, it's Hammer! Who's this?" asked Kurt.

"Hi, Kurt! This is Karl Homme. I know who killed John," said the voice in the telephone.

Karl's voice sounded really distraught.

"Huh? Are you sure?" asked Kurt.

"Yeah, I'm sure. You sound tired," said Karl.

"Yeah, I couldn't sleep. I suspect that I have some kind of insomnia," said Kurt.

"Oh, I understand. Well, can you come and talk with me as soon as you have the strength?" asked Karl.

"I'm coming right away. I'll be there in half an hour," Kurt said and ended the call.

When he had showered and dressed, he went up to the floor above his room to knock on Frank's door, but there was no answer. Kurt knocked another time, but there was still no answer. He decided to call Frank.

"Yeah, hello?" said Frank.

His voice sounded tired.

"Frank, this is Kurt! Where are you?" asked Kurt.

"I'm on the roof! I just decided to grab a few beers," said Frank.

Kurt let out a long and fervent moan and immediately hung up. He continued down on the first floor, out into the reception and then up onto the roof. Frank was sitting at one of the tables under the canopies on the other side. The table looked like a battlefield created by an army of beer bottles. As Kurt walked toward him, Frank was finishing another one.

"Enough," said Kurt firmly.

"I was actually about to go downstairs and go to bed," said Frank.

"Yeah, I'm sure you were," said Kurt sarcastically.

"Is there a special reason why you're up this early?" asked Frank.

"It's already half past eleven. I have to interview Karl Homme. He's the last suspect," said Kurt.

"I can come with you," said Frank.

"You're going to bed — now," said Kurt.

Frank snorted but didn't protest. When Frank got up, he fell across the table's surface, and Kurt had to put his arm around his back and help him down to his room.

"Are you capable of going to bed on your own or do I have to make sure that you'll be alright?," asked Kurt when they stood outside the room.

"I'll get to bed. Tell me how it went when you come back," said Frank as he pulled out a key card from his pants pocket.

"If you're awake," said Kurt.

Kurt walked alone from Pariwana Hostel to José Pardo

Avenue on the edge of the Miraflores district. *I hope he'll manage to find some kind of peace and quiet,* thought Kurt about Frank.

When he reached the hotel, Kurt was reminded why he didn't think that the Dazzler Hotel was especially impressive. The lobby was chocolate-colored and tall, with white columns along the walls. All the furniture was either white or grey. The room was almost empty, except for men in suits here and there who sat with PCs in their laps and phones planted against their ears.

A pianist in a gray Armani suit was playing gentle jazz music performed along one of the walls. He looked as if he had been on a night shift. Light streamed through the two rooftop windows, revealing that the lobby was situated between the hotel's two skyscrapers.

Kurt walked right to the elevator.

When he stood outside Homme's room, he knocked on the door. Nobody opened. Kurt waited a couple of minutes and knocked again. Still no answer.

He picked up his cell phone and called Karl Homme again. Nobody took the call.

"Very strange," concluded Kurt, and he took the elevator down to the lobby again. He walked right past the pianist to the reception, which was built into the same wall where the piano was standing.

"What is it?" asked a friendly lady in her mid-twenties.

"It concerns the person I was going to visit, Karl Homme. He lives on the fifteenth floor, but doesn't answer when I knock on his door. He doesn't answer his phone, despite the fact that he called me exactly half an hour ago," said Kurt.

"Ah, wait a moment," said the friendly lady.

She lifted up the receiving end of a phone in front of her and dialed a number.

After a couple of minutes, she hung up.

"How strange, no answer. Do you think something may have happened?" she asked.

"Have you seen him go out of the lobby during the past half hour?" asked Kurt.

"No," she answered immediately. "But I was in the bathroom for five minutes," she said.

She turned to her colleague, a tall, dark-haired man in his late thirties.

"I haven't seen anyone go out, but a woman checked in," he said.

"What did she look like?" asked Kurt.

The colleague thought for a while.

"It was a tall, blond woman dressed in black," he answered.

"Could you be more specific? How old was she?" asked Kurt.

"She was wearing sunglasses, so it was a bit difficult to decide, but ... the woman was in her mid-twenties, maybe a little younger," he answered.

Kurt's eyes flared.

"Do you remember if the woman had curls?" asked Kurt.

The man thought for a while.

"Maybe a little," he said.

"Did she check in?" asked Kurt.

"No. It could be that she'd checked in earlier. I started my shift twenty minutes ago," said the man.

"Thanks. Could you join me and unlock my friend's room?" said Kurt to the lady.

"Yeah, I guess I could do that, if you fear that something's happened," she said.

"Something's happened?" said the colleague with a fright.

"It is probably nothing. But we ought to check for safety's sake," said the lady.

She turned and came out of a discrete door at the other side of the room, after which she walked toward the elevator and signaled that Kurt should follow.

Kurt couldn't help noticing how short she was. Admittedly, he was taller than the average European, but she was barely tall enough to reach his shoulders, despite her walking in high heels. She smiled widely and walked with a straight back, but not even the most professional mask could hide the insecurity in her gaze. Her tiny doll feet tiptoed nervously across the floor, followed by an uneven rhythm of "click, clack, click, clack." Kurt hoped fervently that nothing had happened. Kurt picked up the cell phone from his pocket and texted a quick message to Alessandra. "Have you been visiting Karl Homme?"

He hoped that the answer would be no. Inside the elevator, Kurt stretched out a hand and presented himself.

"Kurt Hammer, journalist and private eye," he said and smiled comfortably.

"Evy," she said, looking up at him and smiling meekly.

Back on the fifteenth floor, Evy knocked on the door once more. Both held their breath.

Ten seconds.

Twenty seconds.

Thirty seconds.

Fifty seconds.

One minute.

No answer.

"Mr. Homme, are you okay? We're coming in to check up on you," she said.

Evy slid a red key card in the lock by the side of the door. They could hear that the lock on the door opened with a "click."

She opened the door and walked in.

"There's no one in the living room," she said, and Kurt assumed that she meant the bedroom.

But it turned out that Karl Homme lived in a suite. The floor in the hallway was covered in light wood. The roof and walls were completely white.

Kurt took the first the door to the left as he entered the hall and realized that it was locked. "What is in here?" he asked.

"The sauna. You can enter through the bathroom," said her voice from the living room.

Kurt immediately walked to the next door, which turned out to lead into the bathroom. It was completely covered with white tiles. In one corner there was a hot tub and in the other a toilet. Between them was a glass door leading into the sauna.

Inside the sauna, just below the roof, sat Karl Homme, stark naked. His entire skin had a dark blue color. Kurt thought he looked more like an overgrown blueberry than a man. His dark hair, soaked in sweat, was glued to his forehead. His eyes were rolled up in his head so that only the off-white eyeballs were visible.

On the floor of the sauna was a pile of digested food mixed with stomach acid, like some form of human stew, in two different places.

My God, thought Kurt.

"Evy! Come here right away!"

Kurt could hear that she was walking slowly, as if she were afraid of what she was going to see.

When she saw Karl Homme, she exclaimed, "Madre de dios!" Mother of God.

"Help me lift the washing machine," Kurt said.

When they lifted the washing machine, Kurt opened the door. Heat instantly hit them.

"Oh my God. It must be nearly seventy degrees in there," Kurt said.

"How long do you think he's been in there?" Evy asked.

"It's hard to say. But one thing is certain: the one who called me was not Karl Homme. The murderer is trying to send me a message," he said, took off his jacket, and went into the sauna.

"Can you call the police?" Kurt asked.

"Yes, yes, of course," Evy said, putting a hand on her forehead.

Forty minutes later, a knock came on the door.

Kurt opened the door. Sara Sofia Ulo's black eyes pierced through him.

"How did you find him?" she said.

"The sauna is accessible via the bathroom. It wasn't exactly hard," Kurt said.

"Yeah, I don't doubt it," said Sara Sofia, and she walked right past him with long steps.

"Kurt, José. José, Kurt," she said without looking back.

Behind her came a tall man with unruly hair protruding every which way from his scalp. He had a beer gut and a white shirt. On his nose he had a pair of aviator sunglasses from Ray-Ban and under them a huge mustache. He stretched out his hand. On his ring finger he wore a huge gold ring.

"José Ferrara. Coroner," he said.

He spoke almost perfect American English as far as Kurt could hear.

"Kurt Hammer, private investigator and journalist," Kurt said.

"Pleased to meet you," José said.

He followed Sara Sofia straight into the sauna.

"He's been dead for less than twenty-four hours," he noted when Kurt entered.

"How can you tell?" Kurt and Sara Sofia asked in unison.

"Because he has been in a warm place and the body has not yet begun to smell," replied José.

"Are there …" Sara Sofia began.

Her eyes wouldn't leave Kurt's sight.

"One of the receptionists saw two people coming into the reception just over an hour ago," Kurt replied.

"How did they look?" she asked.

"Well, you can go down and talk to him," Kurt suggested.

"Do you have any thoughts about who it may be?" she asked.

"Well, my current theory is that the killer has tried to make it look like one of the people was Alessandra Chavez, the daughter of John Fredly," Kurt said.

"Why do you say that?" asked Sara Sofia.

"What do you mean? I just don't think it was her," he replied.

"Why not?" she asked, scratching her neck.

"A gut feeling," Kurt replied.

"Come and look at this," José said and waved at them with a gloved hand.

Kurt and Sara Sofia came over to him.

"What is it?" asked Sara Sofia.

José pointed to a skin-colored patch on his stomach, next to the navel.

"See? I touched his stomach and got paint on my glove. He is painted blue to make it look like he died of overheating. Most likely he died less than two hours ago. But it is impossible to say for sure until I get him examined in the morgue," José said.

"It must be the receptionist who is the murderer," Kurt said.

"I'll go down to the reception and talk to the receptionist. Do you want to come home with me afterward?" Sara Sofia asked.

"Are you trying to bribe me for my theories?" Kurt replied.

"No. I just wanted see how much integrity you have," said Sara Sofia, kissing him on the cheek and leaving the sauna.

Downstairs on the ground floor, Sara Sofia immediately went over to the front desk and approached the receptionist there. He widened his eyes when he saw her, but she acted like nothing had happened.

"Sara Sofia Ulo," she said, showing him her police badge.

"What can I do for you?" asked the man courteously.

"You explained to my colleague that you'd seen a woman going into the reception. Can you describe her again?" Sara asked.

"She was dressed in black from head to toe. And unusually tall for a woman. I want to say she was about a head taller than you. And she was blond," he added.

Sara thought for a moment. "Do you remember if she returned?"

The man widened his eyes.

"I don't think she actually did," he said.

"So she's still in the hotel," Sara said, taking her cell phone out of her pocket to call for reinforcements.

14

JULY 28, 2014

Felicia Alvdal woke to the shrill sound of her black iPhone 5, which vibrated on the nightstand next to her bed. She turned around tiredly, grabbed it, and realized that the time was 6:15.

"Yes?" Felicia answered.

"Felicia, it's Kurt," the voice said on the phone.

"Yes, I saw that. Are you aware of what time it is?" Felicia asked.

"Around six, isn't it?"

"You should have a very good reason to call me so early, Kurt," replied Felicia.

"Listen! This is important. You must go to Oslo as soon as possible to investigate an address for me. The people I'm looking for now are extremely dangerous, and you have to help me," Kurt said.

"So you expect me to just drop everything and go to Oslo for you?" Felicia asked.

"Listen, Felicia, I can't explain everything, but I'm closing in on the people here and what they've done ... I can promise you two front pages, at least! Talk to Karlsen. He trusts me," Kurt said.

Felicia sighed.

"Okay, I'll call him. You'll hear from me," Felicia said.

"Thank you, dear. I miss you," Kurt said.

"I miss you, too, Kurt. Take care of yourself. Don't get yourself into something too dangerous," Felicia said.

"Hah, thank you," Kurt said.

"By the way, have you managed to make money? Only a week is left until the deadline for paying the medical bill," Felicia said.

"I'm working on the matter," Kurt said.

"Don't work too long, dear. I need you home, not in prison," Felicia said.

Felicia got out of bed and put on her blue denim dress from Stella McCartney, which she had folded neatly and put on the floor. She looked around.

Kurt had withdrawal symptoms the last time he had been lying in this bed. Back then, he trembled like a leaf in a storm in the middle of autumn. She had to hold him until he fell asleep. The next morning, she had to drive him to a new round of treatment. "Never again," she swore at that time.

She went into her small, open kitchen and started her pink K-Mix coffee maker from Jernia. As usual, it had been readied the night before.

Then she looked up Harry Karlsen in the contact list on her phone.

"Hey, Harry! Sorry, I'm calling you so early," Felicia said.

"Oh, I was already up. Didn't sleep tonight. Is there something going on?" Harry asked.

"Yes, Kurt called me from Lima. He's about to solve

John Fredly's murder, but he may already have told you that?" Felicia asked.

"Well, he mentioned it briefly. It seems like he's on his way to getting better. That's what I've focused on," Harry replied.

"Absolutely, and that's great, but he's solving the murder of John Fredly and said he needed help from me. I had to travel to Oslo on the next available flight and seek out an address. He promised me at least two front pages," Felicia said.

"Go! You shouldn't even question it. His nose for news is impeccable," Harry said.

"Well, can I use the business card to pay for the journey?" Felicia asked.

"Yes, go on. Do you need a hotel?" Harry asked.

"You know, I was wondering if I should stay with my sister. Can I get back to you?" Felicia asked.

"No need. If you need to book a hotel room, just pay for it with the card. Good luck," Harry said.

"Thanks, Harry. Stay home. You can appoint Roar to be the functioning editor. He's good," Felicia said.

"I'll think about it. Thanks," Harry said.

Immediately after Felicia had hung up, she called her sister, Maria, in Oslo.

"Hi! I'm sorry to call you so early. Listen, I know this is abrupt, but is there any possibility that I could sleep at your apartment for a night? I can book a hotel, but I thought I should ask," Felicia said.

"Oh, hey, Felicia! Yes, of course you can! When are you coming?" Maria asked.

"I haven't booked a flight yet, but I expect to be there in a couple, maybe three hours," Felicia said.

"Is there anything special going on?" Maria asked.

"I'll explain tonight. Is the key in the same place as always?" Felicia asked.

"Yes, it is, of course. Actually, I was just on my way out the door, so I'll leave it there. Can't wait to see you," Maria said.

"Yes, it will be wonderful! Bye," Felicia said.

Three hours later, she stood in front of the apartment complex where her sister lived. She let herself in with the key hidden in the gutter and moved up to the third floor.

She called Kurt Hammer from her sister's apartment, staring out over Waldemar Thranes Street from behind her sister's large windows.

The apartment only had two rooms, but it was newly refurbished, completely white, and perfect for a person living alone.

"Hi, Kurt," said Felicia.

"Hey, you are alone?" replied Kurt.

"Eh, yes. I'm in Maria's apartment," Felicia said.

"Maria? I don't think she likes me," Kurt said.

"Nonsense. You just drank a little too much the last time you met," Felicia said.

"I was nervous. Wanted to make a good impression," Kurt said.

"What is the address of the apartment?" Felicia asked.

"It's actually not an apartment. I have made an arrangement with the law firm Elden DA in St. Olav's street in Oslo," Kurt said.

"Yeah, okay. What is it about?" asked Felicia.

"It's about John Fredly's will. John had just changed it before he died, and you have to get John Christian Elden to admit it. Sorry you had to go all the way to Oslo, but I needed to make sure you went before I told you. Good luck," Kurt said.

"Elden? Isn't he that celebrity lawyer? And thank you. I think I need it," Felicia said.

"Yes, that's right. Lawyers are tough nuts, but you can probably do a background check on him," Kurt said.

"I'll see what I can do, Kurt."

A few hours later, Maria entered the apartment.

"Mary! Why are you here so early?" Felicia asked.

"I arranged to leave early," Maria replied, coming toward her sister with open arms and a big smile.

Maria resembled her sister so much that they were often asked whether or not they were twins. But Maria had wavy hair and green eyes that always radiated kindness and was definitely the most outgoing of the two.

"It's so good to see you," Felicia exclaimed.

"The same to you, dear. Shall we sit down?" Maria asked.

"Yes, maybe I should tell you why I'm here," admitted Felicia.

"Well, you don't have to," laughed Maria, "but it would be exciting."

"I'm here on a job mission. Kurt needs my help," Felicia said as they were settling into the light brown sofa in the living room.

"Kurt? What has he been entangled in in now?" Maria asked.

"Oh, come on. He's actually not that bad," Felicia said.

"When I first met him, he had to vomit in the toilet and then lie down to sleep for forty minutes," Maria said.

"He was nervous, he was so desperate to give a good first impression. And he's an excellent journalist. He's extremely affectionate," Felicia said.

"So, what's he asked you to do?" Maria asked.

"To ... get information from a lawyer," replied Felicia.

"Huh?" Maria asked.

"I'm not going to do anything illegal. I just have to make him understand how important it is that he gives us this information," Felicia said.

"Do you trust him?" Maria asked.

Felicia hesitated.

"Kurt? Yes, I do," she replied after a while.

"Then I trust him, too," replied Maria. "As long as he doesn't put you at risk."

"Danger is part of my job ... and yours," replied Felicia.

Maria looked into her eyes before she hugged her for a long while.

―――――

THE LAW FIRM Elden DA was situated in a nondescript building with seven floors on St. Olavsgate, a stone's throw away from the Royal Castle. The headquarters of Norway's Legal Association was only two blocks away from the building covered with blue tin plates and brown windowsills. Inside the building, Felicia took the elevator up to the second floor.

The reception had marble floors and a white concrete ceiling. The wall on her right side bent inward in a weak semicircle. In the middle of the wall there was a series of windows that showed the offices in the other room. In the middle of the room, against the elevator, stood a reception desk made from the same light wood as the wall behind it. Next to the counter was an aluminum bench with a black seat, and on the opposite side of the room stood a pair of tables in the same style decorated with green plants. *It's all more reminiscent of a waiting room for a private doctor's office than a law office,* Felicia thought.

Felicia tried to look as if she was full of confidence and went straight to the reception desk. There sat a brunette with brown eyes and hair flowing to her chest. She was elegantly dressed in a gray skirt, a brown belt, and a white blouse. She looked up at Felicia and revealed a chalk-white smile for a few seconds.

"What can I help you with?" asked the brunette.

"Hi, I have an appointment with John Christian Elden right now at 1:00 PM," replied Felicia.

"What's your name?" asked the brunette.

"Felicia Alvdal, but I'm not the one who made the appointment. It's Kurt Hammer," replied Felicia.

"Ah," she said, looking down at the PC screen in front of her. "Let's see ... here you are," she said, looking up again. "I'll call him and ask him to come out."

"Thank you," Felicia said and sat down on the bench. For the occasion, she had put on a black silk dress from Armani and hoped she was looking presentable.

After five minutes, John Christian Elden approached her from a door on the other side of the room. He had short, dark hair and light blue eyes that were quite deep-set. He had a powerful nose and a charming smile. He was dressed in a black, tailored suit from Hilfiger with an accompanying burgundy tie and burgundy silk pocket square in his breast pocket.

"Hey, are you Felicia? Welcome," said John Christian.

"Thank you," Felicia said, getting up and down.

"Should we go into my office?" he asked, stretching out his arm.

"Certainly," replied Felicia, following.

John Christian's office was covered in light green wallpaper while the floor was light gray. His office desk was designed in light brown oak. Behind it, the entire long wall was covered by a window that overlooked the Royal Castle park, in front of which stood a bench in the same light oak as the office desk. The other wall was adorned with pictures of famous places all over the world that had been placed seemingly at random while still avoiding a messy impression.

"Sit," said John Christian, pointing to one of two gray plush chairs placed in front of the desk.

"Thank you," Felicia said and sat down.

John Christian sat in his gray office chair behind the desk.

"So," he said. "What can I help you with?"

"It's about a client of yours. John Fredly," answered Felicia.

"Ah. Very sad case. The family called me a week ago and told me what had happened. I should probably be angry and ask how you even know that he's my client, but now that he's dead, it probably doesn't matter all that much," said John Christian.

"No, I think you're right," admitted Felicia. "We ... that is Kurt and I are investigating John's murder now, and we will probably work together to write a story about it. But I can guarantee you that it won't be a speculative piece. John was a personal friend of Kurt's, and we don't have to mention your name or drag your company into the story if you don't want us to," Felicia said.

"Oh, no, I didn't mean it that way. John was my client, and I have no need to deny it. But John was very fond of his privacy, and if he had been alive, I don't think he'd appreciate it if people were investigating his private life. Anyway, what can I help you with in this matter?" asked John Christian.

"Well, the thing is that Kurt has reason to believe that

John recently changed his will. Kurt never mentioned how he got to know it, but he is a skilled journalist and when he has a suspicion, there's usually something there. We need to know everything we can. Your client is dead, John Christian, and if you care whatsoever, I urge you to help us," replied Felicia.

John Christian sighed.

"Fucking journalists," he said.

He bit his lower lip.

"Sorry, I ... this is a difficult situation," said John Christian.

"I understand that, and I'm so sorry," Felicia said. "But we are only trying to help the family of a deceased client."

"The family, hmm? They were the ones who wanted Kurt to take the case?" John Christian asked.

"Yes," said Felicia.

"Let me check John's will. Do you want to sit here and wait, or do you want to sit in the reception?" asked John Christian.

"Here's fine if you don't mind," Felicia said.

"No problem," he said and rolled over to the PC screen located at the other end of his office desk.

After a few minutes, he rolled back and approached Felicia. "I can say that the last will and testament was recently changed. A few weeks before John died, actually. I can't say more than that, but I'll send a letter to Kurt today. In it I will write the information he needs to know," said John Christian.

"Thank you," Felicia said, getting up and curtseying. "You've been a great help!"

"It was nothing. Just don't write a degrading thing about us or John, because then I'll ruin you," he said.

On her way home to Maria, Kurt called her. "So? How did it go?" he asked.

"He'll send you a letter with everything you need. I expect it to be there in a week," Felicia said.

"Oh, amazing! You've done a great job, Felicia. Are you seeing a story?" Kurt asked.

"Well, I might have imagined that you could help me come up with a headline, since I helped you," replied Felicia.

"I'll see what I can find. I'll send you some suggestions by email tomorrow! Thank you for the help. I miss you," Kurt said.

"I miss you too, Kurt, but maybe you should have a chat with Frank," Felicia said.

15

JULY 29, 2014

Frank Hansen woke up in his double bed. What had awakened him? He looked around in the semi-dark room, with sweat dripping down his back. On the dark brown bedside table, his iPhone 5 vibrated.

The clock on the screen read four in the morning.

"Who the hell's calling this time of day?" Frank wondered.

The number was Norwegian but unknown.

Frank pressed the green button on the screen and held the phone to his ear.

"Frank Hansen?" asked a voice with an accent from Trondheim.

The voice in the other end sounded curious, friendly, and safe.

"Yes, it's me," Frank said.

"Hi, this is the Chief Doctor Karl-Inge Tallaksen from St. Olav's hospital in Trondheim," said the voice.

Frank took a deep breath and let the air out of his lungs slowly.

"What is it?" asked Frank.

"It's about your daughter. Are you alone at the moment?" Karl-Inge asked.

"Yes. I don't need to be around anyone, just say what it is," Frank said.

"Mr. Hansen, I really recommend that you are with a friend or colleague right now," Karl-Inge said.

"Just talk, damn it," Frank said.

"Well, there's no easy way to say this, but ... your daughter died five minutes ago. We did everything we could to revive her, but her heart failed," Karl-Inge said.

Frank couldn't believe it. The words that came from Norway might as well have come from Mercury or Venus.

"You're lying! Stine?! She was stable! I was supposed to be able to visit her in a few days," Frank said.

"I'm very sorry. As we said, we did everything we could. In a coma, the patient's condition can change rapidly," replied Karl-Inge.

Frank ended the conversation. He put down the mobile on the bedside table, swung his legs out of bed and placed them on the bedroom floor.

It felt like it was made of glass and could break into a million pieces at any time, pieces that would pierce the soles of his feet. He could imagine streams flowing from his feet, shaping themselves into a blood-red Nile that slowly but surely filled the room.

He reached out for his gray Dolce & Gabbana shirt on the floor and spent ten minutes putting it over his head and securing the two buttons at his throat. Then he reached out for his black flannel shorts, also D&G, which he had bought yesterday. He spent another ten minutes pulling them up to his waist and buttoning them.

Finally, he picked up his mobile again, started Spotify, and put on the song "Hljóða Nótt" by Ásgeir. Icelandic was not a language he had mastered, but in spite of the barrier, the Icelandic singer's fragile voice vibrated in his soul right now.

When the song was over, Frank found courage and stood up. Immediately, he returned to bed. He pushed his hands hard into the bed and got up again. This time he managed to stand. He bent over and put on his socks and shoes.

With unsteady steps, he walked across the bedroom floor and to the door across the room.

Soon, he stood on the threshold of a bar a few hundred meters from the hostel. He didn't know how he got there, what he was going to do, or how to get back, but a wolf howled in his subconscious mind with a strength and intensity that just begged to be hushed.

A huge security guard, two meters tall and certainly over one hundred kilos, looked at him with skepticism but let him pass by, having stared at him for what felt like an eternity.

Frank ended up on the 19th floor of the Hilton Hotel in the Miraflores district. The combined bar and restaurant on the top floor was located outdoors, with a three hundred and sixty-degree view across Lima. Frank didn't bother noticing, and he walked straight to the bar in the middle of the outdoor area. It was a horseshoe shape made from polished wood, and he was all alone. The bartender looked as though he wanted to go to bed.

"A pint please," Frank said.

The bartender nodded and poured a Carlsberg from the tap.

Usually he would have protested when a beer cost one hundred NOK, but right now he was ready to do anything to still the wolf in his head. He sat alone in one of the purple booths next to the bar. He took two large sips of beer before he put it on the table in front of him and laid his head in his hands. He envisioned the first time he had held Stine in his arms in St. Olav's hospital. He had swung her around the room and let out a laugh warmer than anything he could remember doing before or since. Now he looked out at Lima's illuminated cityscape. All the skyscrapers under a blue-gray sky dissolved into hundreds of fragments of tears flowing down his cheeks.

Frank didn't know how long he'd been sitting there when he was suddenly hit hard in the head by something that felt like a fist.

"You fucking idiot! You slept with her, didn't you?" Kurt shouted.

Frank turned around suddenly, and to his great horror, he saw Kurt Hammer behind him. He looked even taller than usual. He was red in the face, smoking a Marlboro cigarette, and had murder in his eyes. He didn't have time to put on his hat, and his bloodshot eyes indicated that he had been looking for Frank for hours.

"Huh? What? How? Hi, Kurt."

"Don't pretend. You know perfectly well what I mean," Kurt said.

"Kurt, I ... they just called from the hospital. Stine is dead," Frank said.

"Oh, hell. I ..." Kurt said.

Kurt disappeared as soon as he had appeared and was soon back with two beers.

Frank looked at him as he sat down beside him.

"Kurt, you can't drink. You know I can't let you get ..." Frank said.

Kurt sighed. "You're right," he replied.

Trembling, he pushed both beers over to Frank, who

didn't say anything. After a while he was back with a glass of cola.

"Is there rum in that?" Frank asked.

"Haha, very funny," Kurt replied and pushed Frank to the side.

Then he lifted his glass toward Frank and said, "For Stine!"

Frank took up his first glass from the table in front of them and clinked it against Kurt's.

"For Stine," Frank said. Then he sighed. "Kurt, I don't know what you think happened between me and Felicia. Nothing happened. She … tried to kiss me in a weak moment. I let her do it for a while before I realized how wrong it was. Please forgive me," Frank said.

"Don't think about it. I know what it's like to lose someone. The relationship between me and Felicia has been a bit difficult since I left anyway. She didn't want me to go. We hadn't really seen each other while I was receiving treatment. What she doesn't seem to understand is that I came down here to finalize my treatment so I can fully recover and be with her again," Kurt said.

"And how do you think it's working out?" Frank said with a gritty smile.

"Well," Kurt said. "It could be worse. Now I've got so much to do that I don't have time to drink. Speaking of … tomorrow we must go to the Sørdalen couple."

"Oh, I don't know if I can," Frank said.

"You have no choice. I won't let you sit in the hostel drinking," Kurt said.

"Okay, I'll join," Frank sighed. "But I have to call a funeral home and … and …"

Frank let the tears flow. He sobbed and sobbed incessantly.

Kurt put his arms around him and held him tight.

The memories flowed. Kurt remembered it as if it were yesterday. Marte, his wife, the most beautiful creature he could imagine in the whole world, lay in the double bed at home in Volveveien. Her blue eyes were open and looked up at him. Her mouth was stiffened in an open smile, as if she was screaming out for help. Her long, blond hair was sprinkled with blood.

Her stomach, which had given birth to their daughter, was penetrated by dozens of bullets. A tear dripped out of the crook of his eye. He wouldn't wish such a loss on his worst enemy.

Not long afterward, his thoughts flew to Bodø. The last year at the police college. He hadn't heard from John Fredly since that day, or rather he hadn't dared to contact him since then. Two emerald-green eyes, brown bangs, a smile with dimples and the world's most charming laughter had come between them. Janne was her name. Suddenly, she had stood there in front of him, on one of the countless evenings where he had been too drunk to really remember anything. He had stumbled out of some nightclub, probably DamaDi, in a blizzard. Without knowing how, he had been lying at home with her, undressed, in a small three-room apartment in Mørkved. They'd embraced each other.

Suddenly, he had stood there in the doorway: John, his black curls protruding every which way, a witness to the fact that he had been out in the blizzard.

"Kurt, what the hell are you doing here?" John had asked.

Kurt could have looked into anyone else's eyes right then. But not those. Not John's.

He'd gotten dressed at one hell of a speed. The minutes

he'd spent getting out of the apartment were the longest of his life. Outside, he had been met by John.

"How could you?" John had asked.

"I didn't know … I had no idea," Kurt had said.

John had trembled all over his body. Kurt couldn't decide if it was because he was standing without a jacket in minus twenty-five degrees or because he was so angry.

"I've actually been envious of your ability to attract everything that has two legs and a pussy. For once, I had managed to arrange something for myself, and then of all the damn people in the whole universe, you destroyed it," John had cried.

"Why didn't you say anything?" Kurt had asked.

"Maybe because I felt inferior. Had that occurred to you?" John had replied.

"I actually didn't think I had a chance. I'm pretty sure she was the one who came on to me," Kurt had said.

The next second, Kurt had lain in the snow with a bleeding nose.

"Get away! I don't want to see you anymore," John had said, entering the apartment and closing the door behind him.

16

JULY 29 2014

Frank woke up in his room at Pariwana Hostel. The sheets in his double bed had been sticking to his body. Beside the bed his clothes lay in a pile on the floor. He couldn't remember anything from the last few hours, except that Kurt had followed him up to the room some time during the morning.

He looked at his phone; it told him that the time was around half past four.

Then he remembered Stine was dead. He wanted to lie down and cry but decided to grab the phone and call his mother-in-law. "Hi, Grete," said Frank.

"Hey, Frank! How's it going?" Grete asked.

"Pretty miserably to put it mildly. How about you?" he asked.

"I'm still in shock. But I have checked into the hotel here, and I'm here every day while I wait for Alexandra to wake up. I don't know how I'll tell her," Grete replied.

"I'm ... considering coming home. I feel I must be there when she wakes up. And I'm unable to work properly right now anyway," Frank said.

"You have to decide for yourself. But Alexandra hasn't awakened yet. And, of course, I'll call you right away if that happens. The most important thing now is that you take care of yourself," Grete said.

"Thanks. I'll talk to Kurt. I'll call you if I decide to come home. Thanks for being there," Frank said.

"She's my daughter. It's the least I can do," Grete said.

"Still, I appreciate it," Frank said, hanging up.

THE NEXT THING Frank did was dial Kurt.

"Hey, Kurt, it's Frank. Sorry you had to see me like that again. I don't really know how to handle this. I'm considering going home because I don't feel that I'm of any use to you anyway the way I am now," Frank said.

"Frank! I've just finished *Fallen Angels* by Staalesen and thought about going to the Crown Plaza Hotel soon to talk to Jarle Sørdalen."

Silence.

"... but I understand if you just want to be left to mourn," Kurt said.

"Go in advance. Maybe I'll come eventually," Frank said.

"Okay, I hope you'll come," said Kurt.

The Crown Plaza Hotel in the Miraflores district of Lima was one of the gaudiest Kurt had ever seen. Personally, he would never have lived there, at least not based on the first impression. The street façade proudly displayed a kind of modern chandelier that looked suspiciously like a pair of tiger-print underpants against azure blue backlight.

Underneath the gaudy glass façade was "CROWN PLAZA LIMA" written in luminous letters against a black background.

When Kurt had climbed the stairs, he'd heard the sound of a car door that was closed quickly behind him. Out of a taxi came Frank, dressed in a gray hoodie and gray khakis.

"I realized you were right," Frank said before Kurt could open his mouth. Inside the foyer, they were welcomed by Jarle Sørdalen. Kurt was constantly surprised at how small he was; Jarle barely reached up to his shoulder. Still, he made up for it by being immaculately dressed in a tailored, gray, Armani suit. He wore a pair of black Ray-Ban sunglasses as a piece of jewelry attached to his gray shirt under the suit. On his hands he wore black leather gloves.

Jarle met Kurt with a wide smile and outstretched hand. His tiny, brown eyes radiated with extreme self-confidence and a life-long attitude of years without economic boundaries.

"Jarle, this is my colleague Frank Hansen," Kurt said and took Jarle by the hand.

Jarle shot Frank a disapproving look.

"I had a long night yesterday and wanted to wear comfortable clothes. Is there any particular reason why you wear gloves indoors?" Frank asked.

"I've been wearing gloves since primary school. I'm not a fan of bacteria. I was bullied for that, of course, but I made up for it in the schoolyard," Jarle said.

He boxed in the air in front of Frank with a glove-clad fist. Frank avoided rolling his eyes and nodded slowly.

"I think I've read some of your articles in Aftenbladet. You and Kurt wrote about, what was her name ... Olya, didn't you?" Jarle asked.

"Yes, that's right. That one was mostly Kurt, but I helped," Frank said.

"Brilliant, brilliant. Should we sit down?" Jarle asked.

He pointed to four leather chairs and a leather table

that stood on a parquet elevation a little further ahead, flanked by green palm trees.

"Where is Anastasia? We need to talk to her too," Kurt said.

"She's just in the bedroom taking a shower. She's coming soon," Jarle said.

"Anyway. Can we take the conversation inside? Not that I think anyone is going to understand what we are talking about, but it simply feels better to do it there, since we are going to discuss a murder investigation," Kurt said.

Jarle suddenly looked annoyed but quickly recovered. "Yes! It's on the top floor. Let's take the elevator," he said.

The Sørdalen couple's bedroom proved to be a massive suite that contained a terrace, bathroom, combined living room and office, kitchen, and bedroom.

"You live spaciously," said Frank when they came into the hallway and took off their shoes.

"Oh, it was cheap. My hotel chain has partnered with the chain that runs this hotel," Jarle said casually.

The combined living room and office had purple walls with straw-colored carpet. All the furniture was made from light oak. In one corner of the room stood a minimalist office table shaped like a kind of trapeze, where Jarle's laptop sat. In the other corner there was a seating area complete with a sofa and two chairs around a minimalist coffee table. Kurt thought it was pretty boring and looked like any other hotel room in Norway.

"Shall we sit down?" Kurt said, stretching his hand out toward the coffee table.

"Yes, just sit down. I'm just going to go into the bedroom and make sure Anastasia knows we're here," Jarle said.

Jarle went into the bedroom and closed the door behind him, but not powerfully enough to shut it completely.

"What is it?" said Frank when they had sat down.

Kurt's lower lip quivered. His fingers groped the orthodox cross Frank knew he was wearing under his clothes, even though he almost never showed it.

He had learned to read Kurt's smallest mood swings, even when Kurt was quite calm, and everyone thought nothing was happening beneath the surface.

"It's something I don't like. You should have seen Jarle when Karl Homme kissed Anastasia on her hand during dinner. He looked as if he was about going to kill someone. Either he is awfully jealous, or ... " Kurt said.

The sound of something or someone being hit emanated from inside the bedroom.

Frank gasped.

"Stay calm. We can't let him escape now, " Kurt ordered.

Frank nodded gently but looked as if he wanted to choke someone.

A few minutes later, Jarle came out of the bedroom hand in hand with Anastasia. She had twisted her brown, curly hair into a towel on top of her head. Her large, brown eyes shone with a nervousness reminiscent of a terrified horse that had just been put in its place. Her big mouth nevertheless managed to radiate a little smile.

"Anastasia fell in the shower," Jarle said apologetically.

"Is that so?" Kurt asked.

She nodded slightly.

"So you were in the bathroom. Is there a toilet in there?" Kurt asked.

"There is. Why?" Jarle asked.

"Just curious," Kurt said and smiled apologetically.

"Good to see you," Anastasia told Kurt and gave him a long hug.

Kurt shuddered as he thought of what might have caused the sound.

"Can I use your bathroom?" Frank asked.

"Feel at home," Jarle said with no empathy.

"So, where were you on the day when the murder took place, before dinner?" Kurt asked when Frank was back and everyone had sat down.

"We arrived in Lima at around ten o'clock. Then we were driven here to the hotel and arrived about a quarter to twelve, I would estimate. You can ask at reception to be absolutely sure. Then we spent some time unpacking, and I had to do some job-related things while Anastasia took a shower and did women's stuff. We were driven to Plaza Mayor around one o'clock. Then we were shown around the city by a guide and returned to the hotel around six o'clock to get ready for dinner," Jarle said.

"Can you give us the phone number for the guide?" Frank asked.

"Yes," Jarle said.

"You expressed a certain ... annoyance that John bought the paintings by Kandinsky. Did you try to buy them from him?" Kurt asked.

"Hmm. I suggested earlier in the evening, before you came, that I could buy them for 250 million. I said it tongue-in-cheek, but he wouldn't hear talk of it. Do you really think that the paintings could be the motive for John's murder?" Jarle said.

"Well, that's one of the possibilities we're currently investigating. Also, you don't know whether anyone else was trying to buy the paintings, do you?" Kurt asked.

"Well, the Russians, anyway. Aftenbladet wrote about it in that article, in fact, but I haven't had any contact with them, and I don't know anything beyond what I read. John didn't want to hear anything about it. Perhaps understandable, considering that he invited us to dinner just to celebrate the purchase," Jarle said.

"What is your journey's purpose, except for attending the dinner?" Frank asked Anastasia.

She opened her mouth to answer, but Jarle interrupted her.

"Well, when John invited us, we thought we could use it as a kind of vacation. I can work from the hotel room, so this is fine. Anastasia loves to shop, and the plan is to explore the city and attractions together when I'm not working. We had planned to stay here for a week, but if you need us for longer we can probably stay here a few more days. If necessary," Jarle said.

"I'd like to finish the matter as soon as possible, of course. John was my friend, and for my own and the family's sake, I will solve the murder no matter the cost. I can't promise anything, but I'll try not to force you to stay for longer than intended. Can you explain what you saw when you stood on top of the pyramid with John?" Kurt said.

"When John got to the top, he fell down and landed in your lap almost immediately. I just saw the top of his head because Anastasia screamed," said Jarle.

"So there was nothing abnormal happening, as far as you could see?" Frank asked.

"No, unfortunately," Anastasia replied.

Jarle gave her a hateful look.

"Then I think we're pretty much done with the questions, unless you have something you want to add," Kurt said.

"No, we certainly don't," said Jarle.

"Thank you for being helpful," Frank said.

"Don't mention it," said Jarle.

When Kurt and Frank were waiting for the elevator in the corridor outside the suite, Anastasia came running towards them.

"Kurt, Kurt," she said hesitantly.

"What is it, dear?" Kurt said.

"Jarle is going to the bathroom. I don't have much time. If he notices that I have left the apartment, he will come and look for me," Anastasia said.

"Calm down and tell me what you have on your mind," Kurt said.

"Well, Jarle didn't tell the whole truth about why we came here. Before we went to be shown around the city, he was visited by Hugo Friis and Federico Ruez. I didn't know who they were before they introduced themselves at dinner. But Jarle insisted that I shouldn't be in the room while they were here, so I went shopping," Anastasia said.

"And you have no idea what they were doing there?" Kurt asked.

"No, not really. But I think it was a kind of business meeting, because Jarle had put on his purple suit from Dolce & Gabbana, which he only uses in business meetings," Anastasia replied.

"Thank you very much for the information. You've been a great help," Kurt said.

"It was the least I could do," she said, quickly kissing him on the cheek before she disappeared as quickly as she had appeared.

When they were outside the hotel, Frank looked at Kurt.

"Well, that was informative," he said, without sounding completely convinced.

"Yes, it was. By the way, did you notice anything special in their bathroom?" Kurt asked.

Frank thought about it.

"Well, nothing at all, except for unimaginable amounts of makeup. The whole wash basin was surrounded by makeup, and the shelf next to the shower was full of it too," he replied.

Kurt patted Frank on his shoulder.

"Very interesting! You're observant, Frank! But there are still pieces of the puzzle missing. Tomorrow, I suggest that we give the widow a visit. What do you say?" Kurt asked.

"Sounds like a plan," Frank said.

Together they went out into the night and headed back to the Pariwana Hostel.

When the red building that housed the Pariwana Hostel had appeared, Felicia called Kurt.

"Kurt! I've been given another warning that there's only one week left until one of the medical bills goes to the judiciary," she said.

"I'm working on the matter. I'll have it fixed within a week," he said.

"How are you going to fix it?" she asked.

"Just trust me," he said.

"What was that?" Frank asked when Kurt had finished the conversation.

"Just some vultures who are looking to take everything I possess. But don't worry, I have everything under control," Kurt said.

At least I wish I did, he thought to himself.

17

JULY 30, 2014

"Let's go," Kurt shouted.

Kurt knocked on the door to Frank's room and shouted loudly for the second time.

"Yes, yeah, I'm coming," Frank's voice said from within.

When Kurt got up, he had asked Frank if he wanted to go out to have breakfast, but Frank had insisted on being left in peace. Kurt had agreed and had been assured that Frank had no drinks in there.

After five minutes, Frank came out, with bags under his eyes and teary cheeks.

"My God, you look great," noted Kurt.

"Thank you," replied Frank sarcastically.

When they came out to the street, Frank saw that dusk had already settled on Lima, and the streetlights had been turned on. The leaves of the palm trees lining the sidewalk blew meekly with Lima's flag in the roundabout to the right of them.

"How lovely," Frank said.

"Yes, Lima is a nice city. I like it down here. Did you arrange a funeral home?" Kurt asked.

"I did, yes. I have to go home in four days," Frank said.

"Well," Kurt said, "then we don't have much time to solve the case."

"No, we don't. Where does the widow live?" Frank asked.

"She lives at the Courtyard Lima Hotel," Kurt said. "It's a ten-minute walk away."

When they arrived at Calle Schnell 400, it was almost dark outside. The gray-white building that made up the Courtyard Lima Hotel was lit up by neon lights around the windows. The glass façade with the entrance faced diagonally toward the street.

Inside the reception, the floor was made from black marble. Kurt went straight to one of two reception desks designed as semi-circles from light brown wood. He was greeted by a young Peruvian who looked as though she could be in her twenties. Her eyes had a glassy touch, which could only be, Kurt guessed, due to a whole day at work in the service of snobbish tourists.

"Hi there! Can I help you?" said the young lady.

"Can you call Rebecca Swanson? Tell her that Kurt Hammer and Frank Hansen would like to come and ask her some questions," Kurt said.

"Of course! Just a moment," replied the young lady.

The young receptionist hit a number on a telephone behind the counter.

A minute later, the young receptionist put down the phone and said in a gentle tone, "You can just go up! She lives on the fifteenth floor, room O78. You can take the elevator just around the corner."

"Thanks," said Kurt.

When Rebecca Swanson opened the door for them, she wore a green silk dress covered with Swarovski crystals. Her long, red hair was pinned up with a gold brooch, and her green eyes shone like the eyes of a cat that could attack at any time.

A small hallway with white walls led to what was probably a bedroom on one side, and at the end of the hallway there was a white door leading into the living room. The widow's living room had white walls, beige carpet, beige curtains, white ceilings, and a panoramic view of the Miraflores district. In one corner of the room stood a dog basket where there was a small, white poodle.

"Don't worry about Fifi," Rebecca said apologetically. "She wouldn't hurt a fly, except when she's hungry. Then she can become angry."

"Where was she when you were at the dinner party?" Kurt asked.

"Oh, she was here in the room. I got one of the staff to look after her. I had already walked with her. She only needs a short walk a day, fortunately. I don't have the health for more," Rebecca replied.

Her green eyes twinkled, and Kurt could feel what she said was true, even though she was joking about it.

"Sit down," Rebecca said, pointing to a light brown sofa at the other end of the room.

"Thanks," the two said.

"Do you want anything? Coffee, tea, beer?" Rebecca asked.

"Tea," Frank said.

"Coffee," Kurt said.

"Okay, I'll call the front desk. Meanwhile, just sit down," Rebecca said.

Kurt and Frank went to sit down, and from the couch they saw that Rebecca dialed the number to the front desk from her cell phone.

"Yes, hi, it's Rebecca Swanson here. Can I get two black coffees and a tea sent up to my room?" she said.

Silence.

"Yes, put it on my room ... just do it," she said.

Silence.

"Good! Will it take long? No? Good."

When she had hung up, she found a chair and sat down opposite them.

Kurt brought out his iPhone 5, started the recording program, and put it on his lap. He looked at Rebecca, who nodded in agreement.

"What was that?" Kurt asked.

"Oh, nothing. The receptionists occasionally sit on their butts and need some lessons in good manners," she said apologetically.

"And what's all that?" Frank asked, pointing to a bunch of dresses and jewelry lying on the double bed across the room.

"Oh, those are things I no longer use. Thought I should donate them to the poor here," Rebecca said, reluctantly shrugging her shoulders.

Kurt and Frank looked at each other.

"First things first. What is wrong with you?" Kurt said.

"What?" asked Rebecca.

"You said you didn't have the health to go for more than a short walk a day," Kurt said.

"Arthritis. And meningioma," Rebecca said.

"Meningioma?" Kurt asked.

"A brain tumor. I've been extremely unlucky. Ninety percent of meningioma is completely harmless, but mine is of the dangerous type. The doctors have given me two to five years to live. And that's an optimistic estimate," she said.

"Oh. Sorry," Kurt said.

"It's nothing to apologize for. If someone should apologize, it's our lord," Rebecca said, sighing.

Kurt crossed his chest. Rebecca gave him a confused look.

"Are you a Christian, Mr. Hammer?" she asked.

"Not overly. But my dear mother raised me in the orthodox faith, and sometimes I fall back on what she taught me," Kurt said.

"I understand," Rebecca said.

"Can you explain where you were on the day when John was killed? That is, before the dinner party," Kurt stated.

"Yes, of course. I had been home in Oxford to visit my son and arrived at the airport at three o'clock. From there, I was driven to this hotel, where I checked in and slept for a couple of hours. Then I took a shower, walked a little with Fifi, changed clothes, and was driven to the dinner party," Rebecca said.

"But you live here, don't you? Kurt told me you are a tax refugee," Frank said.

Rebecca smiled. "My house is being remodeled at the moment," she replied.

"Do you have any theory on why John was killed?" Kurt asked.

"I thought it was your job to figure that out," Rebecca said sarcastically.

"But now I'm asking you," replied Kurt without hesitating.

Rebecca slowly got up, turned around, and looked out of the windows toward all the buildings in Miraflores.

"Well, he had just purchased two paintings, each of which was worth a small fortune. And the Russians wanted the paintings back, didn't they? I want to say that it was because of the first or second. I was very fond of John, but he shouldn't have bought those paintings. They just spelled trouble," Rebecca said.

"Did you tell him?" Kurt asked.

"No, I didn't have the opportunity to do that. As mentioned, I was back in my home country for a while, and I learned that I was invited to a dinner party on the day of my return to Lima," Rebecca said.

"I think somebody is knocking on the door," Frank said.

"Yes, indeed, I think you are right," Rebecca said, turning and walking toward the doorway. She closed it after her.

As soon as she had done that, Kurt let out a long sigh.

"My God, I never thought she was going to leave the room. See if you find anything suspicious," Kurt told Frank.

"I'm here to write a story, not to engage in illegal theft," Frank said.

"You don't have to take things with you," Kurt said.

Frank reluctantly got up from the chair, walked around the room, and looked around.

Kurt walked over to a phone standing on a brown desk in the corner of the room.

"You have one saved message. Press pound to play it," a voice said on the phone as Kurt pressed some buttons.

Kurt pressed the pound key.

"Rebecca?! This is John Fredly calling! Your threats won't work on me. The paintings are mine and I will keep them."

Kurt shuddered. Hearing the sound of John's voice was like hearing a sigh from a grave.

"What was that?" Frank asked.

"Sounds like Rebecca was willing to do anything to get those paintings," Kurt said.

When she returned, Rebecca had a silver-colored tray with three cups on it. She walked over and put it on a small round table between the light brown chairs next to the double bed. "You have to come over here and take for yourselves," she said apologetically.

When everyone had sat down and sipped coffee and tea, Frank asked, "Have you been interviewed by the police in connection with the death? Can I ask what you said to them?"

"Well, yes, I have," Rebecca said. "There were a couple of young people here who presented themselves as detectives. They wanted to know if I had an alibi, and I said I was present when the murder happened, but ... that there were witnesses that I hadn't done it. I think I mentioned Hugo as a witness," she said.

"Hugo? He wasn't there when the murder happened," Kurt exclaimed.

"Oh, no, how silly of me. Of course. I should have mentioned you as a witness," she said.

"How do you know Hugo?" Kurt asked inquisitively.

"I don't know him as such ... he was John's butler. I often met him when I was visiting John, but nothing more than that," Rebecca said.

"What were you talking about?" Kurt continued.

"When?" Rebecca asked.

"When you met," Kurt continued.

Rebecca hesitated for a moment before she replied, "The weather."

"The weather," Kurt confirmed.

"Yes, it's the sort of thing one talks about when one meets, isn't it?" she asked.

Kurt and Frank looked at each other.

"Can you give an example?" Frank asked.

Rebecca hesitated. "I often said I missed the rain in England. I find it strange to live in a city where it never rains. Hugo often complained that he missed the cold in Norway," she said after a while.

"All right. I think that's everything," Kurt said.

"I hope I was helpful," Rebecca said.

"Oh, undoubtedly," assured Kurt.

Kurt and Frank each took her by the hand before they went and put their cups on the tray and left the room.

In the elevator on the way down to the first floor, Frank concluded, "She's lying!"

"Undoubtedly. But about what?" Kurt said.

"Well, about the clothes on the bed, if nothing else. They're not the sort of garments that you donate to the poor. I bet the average price of those outfits exceeds ten thousand kroner," Frank said eagerly.

"Agreed. Do you know what I think? I think she is bankrupt. When she called for coffee and tea, she had to put it on the room. She lives on empty promises. And I think I know how to prove it," Kurt said.

"What about the relationship with Hugo?" Frank asked.

"There is something that doesn't match up there, too. But it's much harder to prove," Kurt said.

"Why did she mention him as a witness if he was not present during the murder?" Frank asked.

"Simple. Freudian slip. He was the last person she thought of in connection with the murder. Probably because he was the last person she talked to before the dinner party," Kurt concluded.

"Do you think he's the killer?" Frank wondered.

"Obviously not. He was not present," Kurt said as they walked out of the reception and onto the streets of Lima.

Back at the hostel, Kurt called Paul Hammersmith, an old friend from his days of studying in Bodø.

"Hi, Paul! How are you, the kids, and the wife?" Kurt asked.

"Hey, Kurt! Long time no see! We're doing well, thank you. The wife has got a new job as a department manager at a mall."

"You can congratulate her from me. And as regards you ... are you still working for Her Majesty's Revenue and Customs?" Kurt asked.

"Yes, I am. I enjoy working here very much, in fact," Paul said.

"That I understand. No one wanted to owe you a beer in Bodø," Kurt said.

"Haha, you're right. The passive aggressiveness has come in handy lately," Paul said.

Kurt fished out a cigarette from his inner pocket and lit it. The smoke immediately began to flow out toward the open porch of the room.

"You owe me for that time with that guy," Kurt said.

"Oh my God, Kurt. You know I'd do anything for you, but just not at work," said Paul.

"Relax. I just need you to look up a name for me. Rebecca Swanson. Find out if she owes you money," Kurt said.

A long silence followed.

"Is it time sensitive?" Paul asked.

"Hmm. The sooner, the better," Kurt said, ending the conversation.

18

JULY 31, 2014

Kurt's iPhone 5 ringing on the nightstand next to his bed woke him. His eyes flew open at the same time as he cursed the caller. *Who the hell calls this early?* he thought.

He spun around onto his side, yawned, picked up the phone, and noted that it was 9:53. To his great annoyance he realized that he had only slept for two hours before pressing the green button on the screen to accept the call.

"Hammer," he said as gently as he could.

"Kurt, it's Hugo. Listen, John's brother and sister are on their way to Lima. They land at eleven o'clock. They want to make sure the body comes home to Norway. He didn't say why, just that it was what they had come to do," Hugo said.

"Yeah, but what the fuck? They can't do that. The body needs to be examined to find out how he died," said Kurt annoyed.

"There's nothing I can do, Kurt. I just called to warn you," Hugo said.

Kurt counted to ten inside.

"Thank you, Hugo. I'll see what I can do," Kurt said.

He finished the conversation, lifted his quilt, and put on his clothes lying on the floor next to the bed. He ran to the door of the hallway and stormed up the stairs to the floor above, where Frank slept in his room.

"FRANK!" cried Kurt, knocking on the door as he stood outside.

"FRANK!" he screamed again.

Finally, there came a grumpy "What is it?" from inside.

"You have to get up now! We have to meet John's brother and sister at the morgue. They land at eleven o'clock, and we should preferably be there before them," Kurt said.

"What's going on?" Frank asked.

"They have decided to take John's body home," Kurt said.

"What?! Why?" Frank asked.

"Don't know. Just get your ass in gear," Kurt said.

Frank was out of the room in five minutes. His blue eyes were bloodshot, and his short, brown hair looked as if he had just been subjected to a tornado.

"Sleep well?" Kurt asked.

"Haha, very funny. Can we have a coffee to go?" Frank asked.

"They sell coffee at McDonald's across the street," Kurt said.

Frank nodded and together they went to the local edition of the world's most famous fast-food chain.

Already a few minutes after ten, there were a lot of Peruvians waiting in line to raise their blood sugar levels to insane heights before going to work and school.

"My God, I hope they don't come here every day," Frank said.

The smell of deep-frying fat, sweat, and plastic was enough to make him feel like throwing up. The thought of coffee made him endure.

He looked at the Peruvian in front of him in the queue that was two heads shorter than him and twice as wide.

"I sincerely hope they do. I don't want the MC to stop selling fast food to needy journalists and private detectives," Kurt said.

Frank shook his head.

When they had had coffee and breakfast, they hurried together onto the street and into a taxi.

The small, creamy building that housed the morgue in Lima was thirty-five minutes away, on Cangallo Street. The building was surrounded by a black metal fence with concrete columns of the same color as the building. On the roof, the Peruvian flag swayed on the top of a flagpole, and above the entrance to the building was written "MINISTERIO PUBLICO MORGUE CENTRAL DE LIMA" in gold lettering. The building had navy blue moldings and a number of green plants were planted in front of it.

Inside a bland reception, they were greeted by a young lady in her twenties with curly hair and friendly eyes. She smelled faintly of orange and peppermint.

"Hola, puedo ayudarte con algo?" she asked in Spanish. *Hey, can I help you with anything?*

Kurt recognized the tone as gentle and, friendly but at the same time professional. It was a poorly constructed façade to protect oneself from all the horrors one encountered during a workday. It was the type of emotional wall that could drive patients and relatives to the point of breaking, at least those who, in desperation, sought more compassion than one as a professional could afford to give them. He estimated that she had been on the job a few months and was well on her way to finding the right balance.

"We'd like to see John Fredly's body," Kurt said.

"Ah, you are relatives?" she asked.

"No, we are investigating his murder. I think we should be listed as the next of kin," Kurt said.

"Do you have any identification?" she asked.

Kurt and Frank walked over to her and handed her their passports.

"Thanks. Let's see," she said.

She put their names into the MacBook in front of her.

"Here you are. You can simply walk down the stairs to the left of me and straight ahead," she said, smiling.

"Thanks. Has anyone else come to look at him?" Kurt asked.

"No," she said.

"Okay. His brother and sister are coming soon. Can you tell them we're here?" Kurt asked.

"I'll do that," she said.

"Thank you," Kurt said and went down the stairs.

In his career, Kurt had been in different morgues many times, most of them as a police investigator, yet he never quite got used to the experience. There was something about the sterile surroundings, the smell of disinfectant, and the certainty of being surrounded by dead bodies that sent shivers down his spine.

This time was no different. The room had light green floors and whitewashed walls and ceilings. Along each side of the room stood a series of cabinets that Kurt knew contained dead people. The cabinet doors were mostly white but had a strip of aluminum along the top and bottom. Otherwise, the room was dominated by aluminum autopsy tables, each equipped with a separate adjustable lamp hanging from the ceiling.

They were met by a forensic physician, who looked as though he could be in his early fifties. He had an elongated face with a rather pointed chin, very dark almond eyes, and dark hair parted along the right side of his head. His mouth was a straight line, revealing nothing of what was happening inside his head. He was tall and slim, almost as tall as Kurt. He was wearing a white lab coat and light green pants.

"Hi, my name is Alejandro Rodriguez. Who are you looking for?" he asked, stretching out a hand.

"John Fredly," Kurt said.

"Ah, let's see. He's over here," Alejandro said.

Alejandro walked over to the long wall behind them and pulled out a drawer near the floor.

Kurt shuddered at the sight. John's body was completely stiff and ghostly white. His hair was completely flat, lifeless, and hung down the sides of his head.

"Have you had time to look at him?" Kurt asked.

"Haven't had the opportunity, no. The police have needed permission from the family, which they haven't received yet," Alejandro replied.

"Hmm, I understand," Kurt said. "Well, the family is coming here now, so we'll see ..."

Just then, two people came down the stairs from the ground floor.

"Speak of the Devil," Frank said.

The man, who walked in first, came over to them and took Frank by the hand. He was nearly two feet taller and had John's curly hair, only this man's hair was blond, greasy, and grew in every possible direction. His eyes were small and blue. His gaze flickered. His feet were stuck in black platform shoes, apparently made from crocodile skin. *Had he been wearing a black t-shirt and ripped jeans, he'd look like a rock star from the mid-eighties with a cocaine addiction,* Frank thought. But the man was dressed in dark pants and a dark shirt.

Behind him came a woman who seemed to be a few years younger. She was almost two heads shorter than him and had long, curly, black hair. She had blue eyes, thin red lips, and a pessimistic facial expression.

"Hi, Jonas Fredly," the man said and stretched out his hand to Frank. "I'm John's younger brother. This is my sister Linn," he said, pointing to the woman. "Are you Kurt Hammer?"

"No, I'm his colleague Frank Hansen," Frank said.

"Hi, I'm Kurt," Kurt said, turning and stretching out his hand.

Jonas balked, apparently not accustomed to meeting a person who was taller than himself.

"We're here to retrieve our brother's body. Don't get me wrong, as far as I'm concerned you could have examined him for as long as you wanted, but unfortunately our mother has suffered a stroke. I'm afraid John's death took her somewhat by surprise. He was her favorite child. All the while he was the only one with a modicum of talent in the family," Jonas said.

"Please stop, Jonas," Linn said.

Linn looked at him as if he had completely gone off the rails. She came over, shook him, and looked him in his eyes.

"Well, well. The doctors have said that she's recovering, but she has stated that she wants to see John's body and bury it. It is a wish we feel we must respect, in case her situation worsens," Jonas said.

Linn said nothing but nodded firmly and turned to Kurt again.

Kurt said nothing but let Frank talk. Frank went and stood before Jonas and looked into his eyes.

"Excuse me, what is your profession?" he asked.

"Author, with a very modest career. Why?" Jonas replied.

"That's good. Then hopefully you have above average compassion," Frank said.

He cleared his throat, closed his eyes for a few seconds, opened them again, and continued.

"Listen ... I've just lost my firstborn daughter. It is ... to be honest, it is completely fucked up," he said.

Tears formed in his eyes. He looked down for a moment and held his head in his hands.

"I'll never get over it, and the only reason I stand in front of you now is because Kurt needs me. And you need him. Kurt wants to find out who killed a dear friend of his, a friend who happened to be your brother. It should therefore also be in your interest. Believe me, I would do everything in my power to find out who killed Stine. But she wasn't killed. Therefore, I have to live with the blame and shame for the rest of my life. You don't have to," Frank said.

Jonas sighed.

Linn turned to Frank. "Believe me, I also want to find out who killed John. He was my big brother, and I will miss him for the rest of my life," she said.

She spun a few strands of hair around her right index finger, as if to emphasize how much this conversation plagued her.

"But at the same time I just lost my big brother, I can't lose my mother too. I just can't," she continued.

"All we need is a few days. Your mother won't die by that time, and if she does, it doesn't matter if we are allowed to investigate him," Frank said sincerely.

"How dare you!" Jonas yelled.

"He's right," Linn said.

She had to physically hold her brother back to prevent him from getting to Frank.

When Jonas finally calmed down, he said, "Okay. We'll retreat to the hotel to think about it for a day. But don't take anything for granted!"

Kurt nodded happily.

"Can we at least get a blood sample from him? This is no easy case, and I suspect he wasn't shot," he said.

"What makes you believe that?" asked Linn.

"Well, I barely had time to investigate him right after he practically landed in my lap. And if I may ..." Kurt said.

Kurt stretched out a hand to Alejandro, who was on the other side of John's body. Alejandro took the hint and immediately gave him a blue plastic glove from a box on the wall.

Kurt lifted the light green hospital gown that covered the body.

"Here, you see the entrance wound. It is crescent-shaped, and just below his heart. It doesn't look like a bullet wound. More like someone has stabbed him with a potato peeler or the like," Kurt said.

"I agree," Alejandro said.

He looked suspiciously at the wound.

"And look here. Don't close the shirt," he said.

Alejandro ran to a desk at the other end of the room and returned with pliers in one hand. He took it gently to the wound and picked up a couple of strands of hair. "These could be from John or they may originate from the one who inflicted it on him," Alejandro said.

Linn and Jonas looked at each other.

"Interesting theory. Well, I guess it can't hurt if you take a blood sample. But you can't start looking for bullets or the like," Jonas said.

"Glorious. Thank you very much," Kurt said.

When Jonas and Linn had gone, Frank asked, "Why didn't you tell me you didn't think he was shot?"

"Because you never asked," Kurt replied.

"Kurt, I'm here to write a story. You must tell me such things," Frank said.

"Well, you know it now. Do you need help writing the story?" Kurt asked.

"No, you can't write it. You're investigating the case. Besides, I need to take my mind off Stine right now," replied Frank.

"It sounds like a good idea," Kurt said.

Finally he approached Alejandro and asked, "Can you take a blood sample?"

"Yes, of course," answered Alejandro.

"Can you analyze it too?" Kurt asked.

"It depends on what you want to track," answered Alejandro.

"Everything possible, really. But primarily toxins. If you give me the blood sample, I can send it to a private company I know of in Lima," Kurt replied.

Alejandro took out a large needle from his coat, and a few minutes later Kurt had received a transparent container of blood.

"Let's go. Thanks for the help. Remember to tell us if Jonas and Linn show up," Kurt said.

"I'll do that," Alejandro said.

Frank sighed slowly as he and Kurt stood out on the street again.

"That was helpful," he said sarcastically.

"There, there. We just have to cross our fingers that they'll let Alejandro examine the body as soon as possible," Kurt said.

- PROBABLY WASN'T SHOT
BY FRANK HANSEN AND FELICIA ALVDAL

Journalist Kurt Hammer, also at the moment an investigator in the case, has a theory of how famous shipping magnate John Fredly was killed in Lima, the city where he stayed for the last few years of his life. Or at least how he wasn't killed:

"He was probably not shot," was Hammer's preliminary conclusion.

Hammer believes that the wound, which is just below the heart, is not consistent with a gunshot wound. Out of respect for the family, Aftenbladet cannot publish a picture. But we have shown it to forensic scientist, Torleiv Ole Rognum, who, among other things, worked on the July 22 case. He mostly agrees with Kurt Hammer.

"If this is a gunshot wound, I will be very surprised. This looks like a wound from some cutting weapon," he says. "Since it is also just below the heart, it was probably not the one that killed him either."

Uncertain

Hammer admits to Aftenbladet that he is still unsure of who killed Fredly.

"Yes, I am, but I come closer and closer to an answer every day I work on this case. For my own sake, and especially for the family, it is important for me to find the culprit."

Was killed

Fredly was definitely killed, but that's the only thing Hammer and Lima police agree on.

"We still have all the cards on the table," says Carlos Martinez, Lima's police investigator.

Fredly's family believes that the police in Lima are corrupt and therefore wanted Hammer to try to resolve the matter.

"These are completely unfounded accusations," says Martinez. "I wonder what motives they have to say that we can be bought. All we want is to make sure the right murderer is brought to justice, and I hope that Hammer will also try to achieve that."

19

AUGUST 1, 2014

"Frank, Karl Homme's dead," Kurt said over the phone.

Frank sat at a Starbucks cafe a few hundred yards away from the hostel and tried to cure the worst headache of all time with a venti latte and a cheese and ham croissant.

"I have to talk to Alessandra again. The receptionist at Dazzler Hotel says he saw a woman resembling her going in through the reception one hour before I found him dead. She denies that it was her, but I've agreed to meet her. I would appreciate it if you were there," Kurt said.

Frank noticed that he didn't really have any desire or strength, but when he thought about it, there was no point in pretending to be better off sitting in the hostel without doing anything either. He just wanted to fall back to drinking or at best crying himself to sleep.

That morning he had put his feet on the floor and noticed that his legs felt like they were made of rubber. With a lot of difficulty, he picked up his pants from the floor and pulled them on. His hands and legs were shaking. He spent five minutes buttoning his pants.

He sighed.

He pulled up the white flannel shirt from the floor, put it on, and spent ten minutes buttoning two buttons. He couldn't do more. He stuffed his shirt into his pants before he put on his socks from the floor and shoved his feet into his shoes.

When he had finished eating his breakfast at Starbucks, he went out into the street and found a taxi.

Forty minutes later, he stood in front of a building sectioned into apartments of various sizes in different colors. Some were pink, others were light blue with rusty red frames, others were burgundy, and others were white. He didn't manage to find an entrance, but after walking around the building a couple of times, he finally found a gate painted in screaming yellow that led him into a courtyard. From there he went up a purple staircase and knocked on a pink door marked "Numero 201."

It was Alessandra who opened the door. She looked him up and down without saying a word.

Frank sighed.

"I just got up," he said honestly.

"Come in. Kurt is already here," she said.

Frank nodded and followed her into a narrow, light corridor with blue patchwork carpet and large mirrors on the walls. He took off his shoes and followed her further into the kitchen. Kurt sat at the table that looked like it was bought at a flea market. The whole decor looked as if it had originated from the mid-fifties, early sixties. Frank sat down next to Kurt, and Alessandra settled on the other side of the table.

"Colombian coffee?" she asked, looking at Frank.

"Certainly," Frank said.

She turned and picked up a metal can from the kitchen counter, which she handed to Frank.

"So, you weren't at Hotel Dazzler an hour before I found Karl Homme dead there?" Kurt asked.

"No, I wasn't, as I wrote in the message I sent you," answered Alessandra.

"Do you have anyone who can confirm it?" Frank asked.

"Hugo can confirm it. I was in Casa Aliaga at work, and when I got the message from Kurt, I asked if I could get time off to meet him. I don't really live here anymore, but I still have the key to the apartment. I occasionally look after Tricia's dog," Alessandra replied.

As she said it, a small, white chihuahua with brown spots and big eyes walked into the kitchen.

"Speak of the Devil. There he is. Isn't he sweet?" Alessandra asked, lifting him up in his lap.

"The last time we met you we were in your new home, Casa Aliaga, and Hugo insisted there had been an episode the night before John died," Kurt said.

"An episode?" asked Alessandra.

"Yes, his impression was that you had locked yourself in John's room during the night. He thought it could only have been you, since only you and he have a key to John's room. Nothing illegal happened. He checked carefully if something was missing in the morning, but couldn't find anything," Kurt said.

"Had," said Alessandra.

"Excuse me," Kurt said.

"We don't have the key to the room anymore. We had to give them to the police the day after John was ..."

Tears appeared in Alessandra's eyes, and her body began to shiver. Neither Kurt nor Frank said anything, but

Frank took her hand and held it in his. After a minute, she exclaimed, "I'm alright," and took away her hand.

"The police have admittedly only been there a couple of times in retrospect, apparently for the sake of investigating for the most part. But we still don't have keys until the case is closed. Could Hugo confirm that he had seen someone there?" asked Alessandra.

"No, but he insisted he heard someone in there," Kurt said.

At once she became quiet and concise and straightened her back. "Well, it wasn't me," said Alessandra.

Kurt sighed.

"A person who attended John's dinner party has just been murdered. And it most likely was done to send me a message. It is becoming clearer and clearer that we are dealing with someone who is willing to do anything to get away with it. If you care about your life and mine, you'll tell me the whole truth," Kurt said.

Alessandra collapsed in the chair but didn't spend much time straightening up.

"I wasn't there, I've said. John was ..."

"Yes," Kurt said.

Alessandra shook her head. "I loved him very much. He was not just an employer for me but a dear friend. I have nothing to gain from lying," she said.

"Then we have nothing more to talk about," Kurt said.

"Sorry, I couldn't help," said Alessandra.

Kurt got up and signaled to Frank that he should follow.

"Wait," said Alessandra when Kurt stood in the doorway.

Kurt turned around and looked at her without saying a word.

"I noticed something the day John was killed," whispered Alessandra.

"Huh?" Kurt said.

"I noticed something the day John was killed," Alexandra said, a little louder now.

Kurt came back and sat down, still without saying a word.

"I was in the kitchen a few hours before dinner in Huaca Pucllana," Alessandra said.

"Chef Federico Ruez was cooking. I had been told by Hugo to go and hear if he needed any help, but he didn't. When I was about to leave, I noticed white flowers in a transparent vase standing on one of the kitchen counters. I asked Federico what kind of flowers they were, but he just shrugged his shoulders and said he liked to pick flowers. Since I hadn't seen flowers in the kitchen before, I thought it was very strange, so I took a picture of them. They were pretty nice flowers," said Alessandra.

"Can you show me the picture you took?" Kurt asked.

Alessandra took out her mobile phone from her pocket and after a bit of scrolling, she gave it to Kurt.

"Oh my God. Frank, you have to come see," Kurt said.

Frank bent over the table, and Kurt showed him the cell phone.

"Is that what I think it is?" Frank asked.

"I'm afraid so," replied Kurt.

On the way home to Pariwana Hostel, Kurt's mobile phone chimed.

"Hammer speaking," Kurt said.

"Hey, Hammer, it's Jonas Fredly. Our mother just died," Jonas said.

Kurt stopped.

"I'm sorry," he said.

"Thanks. You can tell that ... Alejandro was that what he was called? ... that he can investigate John. Just make sure he's patched up again afterward so he can get a worthy burial," said Jonas.

"Of course, Jonas. It ... he was my friend. That's the least I can do," Kurt said.

Kurt hung up, sat on a bench, took out a pack of Marlboro Golds from his shirt pocket, and lit a cigarette.

Maybe this case is finally drawing to a close, he thought as he breathed in and looked over Lima's skyscrapers.

20

AUGUST 1, 2014

"Where am I?" asked Alessandra Chavez.

She sat in a room and was almost blinded by the sunlight that hit her eyes. It came in from an open window that what seemed like the first sunbeams of the day had fallen in love with. Steven Tyler of Aerosmith, Ozzy Osbourne, Metallica, Nirvana, Led Zeppelin, and Slash looked down at her from the walls.

"In the boys' room. More precisely, on Strindheim in Trondheim," said a friendly voice behind her.

She turned abruptly. Behind her, sitting on a duvet cover adorned with the iconic logo of Metallica, was John Fredly, looking at her. He smiled.

Somehow, he looked younger than she remembered him. He had not changed significantly, but the facial features were less aged, and he didn't seem overworked or stressed. He didn't wear his black glasses. His tight curls were still neat and delicate in a bundle on top of the head, but his hair was shorter than she could remember. Now he looked straight at her with his blue eyes, which stood in stark contrast to his black, curly hair. His nose looked exactly like her own, right down to the flat bridge she had never liked on her own nose, but which looked so attractive on him.

Alessandra noticed a family photograph on the nightstand. The family seemed to be on holiday in southern Europe somewhere, flanked by palm trees, sun, and blue skies. A woman with long, blond hair and corkscrew curls stood behind and smiled at the camera. She had friendly facial features, eyes shining like two blue diamonds in her face, and she wore a blue dress. Beside her stood a man who was a head taller. He had two rings in each ear. His hair was as black as the clothes he was wearing and had grown past his shoulders. He wore dark sunglasses, and Alessandra thought he looked like a rock star. In front of them stood three children, two boys and a girl. She recognized one of them as John. The other boy had long hair like his father, but his hair was blond like his mother's. He stood almost two heads above the other kids and was dressed in a white t-shirt and surfer shorts. The girl had long black hair, thin red lips, and a scowl on her face.

"Is that ... your family? My family," Alessandra asked, pointing to the picture.

"It was an idiotic compromise with Mom. I had to hang that picture there to be allowed to have the posters on the walls," John apologized.

"Are they still alive?" Alessandra asked.

John shrugged.

"This is ... your room? Where you grew up?" asked Alessandra with a trembling voice.

"That's right," John said. He smiled. His pearly whites flashing toward her.

"Are you real?" she asked.

"I'm sitting here, right in front of you, aren't I?" he replied rhetorically.

"Why did you leave Mom and me? Why didn't you ever come back?" she asked.

"I had to go home and finish my studies. I didn't know you existed! And I came back, didn't I?"

"But you didn't let me know," she said, a little indignantly.

"And that," he said, taking a break for posterity, "can be said for you too."

Alessandra felt tears coming.

"I ... it wasn't my responsibility! It wasn't me who went and died," she said with a shrill voice.

"I wasn't supposed to die, dear. Life is unpredictable. I wasn't supposed to have you either, but that doesn't mean I wouldn't have wanted to spend more time with you," he replied.

"I hate you," said Alessandra, and she burst into tears.

"I love you," John said.

"Daddy," she said loudly, stood up from the chair she was sitting on, and ran towards him.

As she threw herself around John's neck, she opened her eyes.

She lay in her own bed and rose abruptly. As she lay down again, she realized that her pillow was completely soaked in sweat.

"Dad," she screamed with the full power of her lungs.

There was no answer.

21

AUGUST 2, 2014

On the way to Jorge Chavez Airport, Frank noticed that the taxi he was sitting in was moving at a snail's pace past the port city of Callao. He suddenly remembered that it was here that Thor Heyerdahl back in the forties had started his journey to Polynesia with the fleet Kon Tiki. He looked at the clock and realized that he still had over two hours until the plane to Texas was leaving Lima.

"Stop here," he said.

The driver, a small, bald man with a big mustache, turned around in his seat and asked, "Here?"

"Take me to La Punta," Frank said.

The taxi driver shook his head but took off to the right.

"Plaza Miguel Grau?" asked the driver.

Frank didn't know where he meant, but just nodded his head.

Ten minutes later, he was released into a place overlooking the sea. A large statue of a highly decorated man pointing out to the sea on top of a marble column dominated the square. Frank walked over to a row of canons and looked out to sea. In his outer vision, he had a series of red and white cranes and a bunch of containers. *Out there somewhere*, he thought, *is Polynesia*.

He wondered if Thor Heyerdahl had ever considered turning around, either because he was scared or because he simply felt like just giving up.

On the other side of the city, Kurt Hammer was on his way to Casa Aliaga. He sat in a black taxi with yellow and black checkers on its sides and cursed Lima's constant traffic jams. "How long will this take?" he asked in a bit of unconfident Spanish. "Maybe half an hour," answered the middle-aged driver, who shrugged.

Since he landed in Lima and became involved in the murder investigation of his former best friend, Kurt Hammer hadn't thought about the odds that someone would want to take his life. Therefore, it was also these odds more than anything else that surprised him when a roar reminiscent of a swarm of oversized, angry wasps occupied the sonic space inside and around the taxi. Two black motorcycles appeared on either side of it. He managed to register that the Japanese rice rockets were Kawasaki Ninja H2s. The drivers were dressed in black leather suits and wore black helmets with black visors. Behind them sat people with machine guns, also dressed in black leather suits and black helmets. In a matter of seconds, they fired a number of shots against the taxi and disappeared in the direction of Lima center. The sound drowned out the traffic and was reminiscent of the sound of thunder in the rain season.

"Are you alright?" Kurt asked.

There was no answer.

Kurt took a quick look at the driver in the front seat and noted that he had been hit in the chest and that his face was completely deformed. Kurt's hair was stained with blood, and he could feel a strong pain in his left leg.

My God, I have to get to hospital, thought Kurt.

He folded his hands around the small silver cross he that had hung around his neck ever since his mother baptized him in the Russian Orthodox Church as a child. Then he closed his eyes and said a quick prayer in Russian.

He opened the door, noticed that it was full of bullet holes and that it was very difficult to walk on his left leg.

"Hey, do you need a ride," said a well-known voice behind him.

He turned around and discovered that Sara Sofia Ulo leaned out of the window of a black car behind him. Her black hair blew in the wind.

"My God, what are you doing here?" Kurt asked.

"I was on my way to Casa Aliaga to talk to ..."

"The same person as me?" Kurt asked.

"Yes, exactly. Jump in," she said.

Kurt hobbled over to her car and jumped into the passenger seat.

"Unfortunately, trying to follow them in this traffic is useless, but I've sent out a message on the radio," Sara Sofia said.

"They had folded registration signs," Kurt replied.

"I know. Hopefully, there are some people who'll spot them. You were lucky. See if there is anything in the backseat that you can use to stop the bleeding," said Sara Sofia.

"Is this what I think it is?" Kurt asked.

He noticed the characteristic wing-shaped logo of the car manufacturer, Aston Martin, on the wheel.

"It's a Vanquish S, yes," replied Sara Sofia.

"It's not your car, is it?" Kurt asked.

"Hah, I drive a motorcycle," replied Sara Sofia.

"Me too," Kurt said, grinning.

"We are collaborating with the Guardia Civil on a case, so we borrow some of their cars. This one is such a good drive that I could almost consider replacing my bike," Sara said, grinning.

Kurt looked behind him and didn't notice anything.

"The backseat is empty," he noted.

"¡Mierda! Here, take this," Sara Sofia said.

She took off her pantyhose and gave it to Kurt.

"I hope you have something under there," Kurt said.

"Just tie it as hard as you can around your calf," Sara Sofia said without commenting on the innuendo in Kurt's voice.

"Are you sure there was no blue light behind there?" she continued.

Kurt turned around and looked again. Sure enough, there was a blue light on the floor.

"There is, actually, but I can't get to it," Kurt said.

Sara Sofia took off her seat belt around her waist, turned, and picked up the blue light from the floor.

Soon they were driving on the highway between two rows of cars pulling aside to leave them free get to the nearest hospital as soon as possible.

"Can you get out of the car on your own?" Sara Sofia asked as she stopped outside Clinica Javier Pardo.

Kurt didn't have time to answer before Sara Sofia had hurried out of the car, walked around, opened the door on Kurt's side of the car, and grabbed his arm.

After hobbling up to the reception closely entwined with Sara Sofia, Kurt was immediately put on a stretcher. Sara Sofia bent down, tucking black hair behind her ear, and kissed him on the forehead before he was rolled into an operating room. After a few hours, the sun had gone down and Kurt woke up from the general anesthetic in a single room. He looked right into Frank's blue eyes.

"What are you doing here? Am I dreaming?" Kurt asked.

A major wrinkle had formed between Frank's eyebrows.

"I changed my mind. I was on my way back when I was called by Sara Sofia. She said you were hospitalized, and I got a feeling of déja vu."

"What about Stine?" Kurt asked.

Tears swelled in Frank's brown eyes, but he quickly wiped them away.

"Stine can wait a week," Frank said.

Kurt grabbed Frank's hand and held it in an iron grip.

"That's good. Then I'll have the opportunity to attend the funeral, hopefully together with Felicia," Kurt said.

"I would appreciate it if you showed up, but first of all you need to concentrate on getting well," Frank said.

"Oh, I was just hit in the left leg. I'll be back in a couple of days or so. I don't know if Sara Sofia told you, but we agreed upon how to catch the killer. Now we know who did it," Kurt said.

22

AUGUST 3, 2014

Kurt Hammer arrived at the Presbitero Maestro cemetery on crutches together with Frank. The cemetery was filled to the brim with statues, mostly made from white or gray marble. Some of them represented the Virgin Mary, others angels, and others naked men who sat with their elbows on their knees, looking down into the ground in front of them.

John Fredly's coffin was open and placed on a small grass spot between two short palm trees. Alessandra Chavez and what seemed to be her mother had already arrived, in addition to Hugo, Jonas Fredly, Linn Fredly, and Mrs. Swanson.

"I thought he was going to be buried at home in Norway," Kurt said to Jonas when he and Frank had arrived at the coffin.

"He was, but Alessandra called us and asked if we could arrange a memorial service here. According to the local tradition, the body should lie in an open chest for three days, preferably covered by blossoms from family and friends," Jonas said.

"We don't have flowers with us," Frank said.

"It's fine. Linn and I have bought a few, as you can see. And Alessandra was kind and brought three big bouquets," Jonas said.

"Did she say why?" Frank asked.

"No, but I guess she just loved her boss," Jonas replied.

"My God, how hot it is?" Kurt said, wiping his forehead with the sleeve on his newly purchased suit.

It was a gray suit, but the fit was the work of a local tailor. He knew that it wasn't an actual Armani, but he didn't care as long as it looked good.

"Winter is leaving us. The temperature begins to rise from mid-August until February," Hugo said.

"Then it's time to resolve this case and go home soon," Frank said.

"Agreed. I didn't come down here to melt away," Kurt said.

"I really hope you find the killers," Hugo said.

"Did you just say, 'the killers,' plural?" Kurt said to Hugo and gave him a suspicious look.

"Yes, I expect no one could have carried out the murder on their own," Hugo said.

Frank and Kurt looked at each other but said nothing.

Kurt leaned over to the open coffin, where Alessandra stood and looked down.

"What happened?" said Alessandra without looking at Kurt.

"I was attacked yesterday, in a taxi. It was a pure coincidence that I survived. An innocent man lost his life and it could have been avoided," Kurt said.

Kurt looked down at the dead body of his good friend. The hair was a bit flatter than Kurt remembered, and John Fredly would never have been found folding his hands over his chest while he was alive. But apart from that, there was nothing about his bodily presence that suggested he was dead. He was wearing a dark suit and had his green cotton scarf around his neck.

Alessandra became white as snow.

"I'll ask you one last time. What was your relationship with John?" Kurt asked.

Alessandra swallowed.

"He was a good friend and employer," said Alessandra.

"And that was all?" Kurt asked, looking down at the sea of roses surrounding the dead body of John Fredly.

"That was all," replied Alessandra Chavez.

"I'm disappointed in you," Kurt said, turning around.

He began to move in the direction he had come before he stopped.

"John's brother and sister are here. You may want to go and say hello. What is your mother's name?" he asked without looking at her.

"Agatha," replied Alessandra.

Agatha Chavez stood a long way from the others and considered her daughter.

She had chocolate-brown eyes, coal-black hair that reached her shoulders, and was a head shorter than her daughter. The only thing she had in common with Alessandra, as far as Kurt could see, was rosy red cheeks and large, fleshy lips. Her eyebrows hung down and gave her a sad facial expression.

Kurt limped over to Agatha.

"Kurt Hammer. Journalist and former police," he said.

She didn't answer.

"I was a friend of John Fredly. Did you tell him about her?" Kurt asked.

Agatha looked at him with teary eyes.

"Does it matter now? He's dead," she said.

"Ms. Chavez, I'm trying to figure out who's behind the murder. Whoever is behind the murder of John is desperate and willing to do anything to escape," Kurt said.

"Are you trying to say that more innocent people can die, Mr. Hammer?" Agatha asked.

"Yes, if you don't tell me what I want to know. I was about to be killed yesterday because your daughter didn't tell me the truth. Did you tell him about her?" he asked again.

"No. No, I didn't. He didn't know anything," Agatha said, turning away.

Jonas and Linn were looking at the coffin that held their late brother when someone tapped Jonas carefully on his shoulder.

Linn was dressed in a short, strapless black dress. On her head she wore a small, flat hat with black mesh that stretched in front of her eyes and nose. Her lips were painted blood red, and her facial expression was more pessimistic than usual.

Jonas had barely squeezed himself into what had to be a tailored black suit. The pants could fit a giant. Around his neck he wore a black bow with sequins. Under the suit he wore a black shirt, and for the occasion, he had put his feet in a pair of black lacquer shoes the size of tennis rackets.

He turned suddenly and looked into the blue eyes of Alessandra Chavez. *Haven't I have seen those eyes before, somewhere?* he thought.

"Hi, Jonas, so sorry for your loss," said Alessandra.

She was dressed in a long-sleeved silk top and a black skirt. In her curly hair she had placed a black clip.

"Hey, how are you doing?" Jonas asked.

Alessandra looked down.

"I'm okay. I was wondering ... how was John, as a brother?" she asked.

"Self-centered," Jonas said briefly.

"Stop it! You'll have to excuse him. He's just jealous. John was the loveliest and most generous brother you can imagine. When I was born, he had saved money and bought a blue teddy bear for me. I still have it," said Linn, smiling.

"He bought two paintings worth millions and held a dinner party to celebrate, but did he invite us? No, we had to read about it in the papers," Jonas said.

"I think ... I think he was envious of you. He never said that he had brothers and sisters, but I got the impression that he had no interest in returning to Norway before ... Well, I don't know what he was trying to achieve. But whatever it was, I got the impression that he didn't feel like he could return before he'd achieved it," said Alessandra.

Jonas turned to John's coffin. He pounded on it so hard that Alessandra thought he would overturn it. Then he raised his arms.

"You idiot, John! Do you hear me? You fucking idiot," he yelled.

When he turned to her again, he had tears in his eyes.

"Sorry. I have to go back to the hotel," he said.

"What was that?" Alessandra asked.

Linn shrugged her shoulders.

"He's a writer. He's always been sensitive," she apologized.

"Is your mother still alive?" Alessandra asked.

Linn looked down.

"She died a few days ago," she said.

"Oh no. Sorry," Alessandra said.

She walked over to Linn and put her arms around her.

"She'll be buried with John when we get home. Actually, I'm glad she didn't live long. I think it was the grief that eventually killed her," said Linn.

"Is there anything I can do?" asked Alessandra when she let Linn out of her arms.

"No, I do not think so. But thank you for asking. I should probably go now. Jonas doesn't like being alone for too long when he's like this," she said.

"I understand," said Alessandra.

She walked over to John's body and kissed him on the forehead.

"Te extraño tanto," she said. *I miss you so much.*

23

AUGUST 4, 2014

"Why has he invited us here?" Jarle asked.

Anastasia and Jarle Sørdalen stood outside Casa Aliaga, speaking to Hugo Friis. Outside, it rained for the first time in 2014.

"He wanted to talk to everyone in the same room," Hugo said. "I said he could use the house."

Jarle scratched his slippery chin.

"I understand. Well, we'll go up to hear what he has to say," he said.

"I'll be with you," Hugo said. "He wanted to make sure I was going to be there too."

Kurt Hammer had dressed in his newly purchased suit for the occasion. In the breast pocket he had placed a red rose. He had put on polished black shoes and stood upright with the help of a pair of crutches.

"Ah," said Kurt to Jarle, Anastasia, and Hugo as they entered the living room on the second floor. "Everyone's here. Sit down!"

He pointed to three empty chairs made from dark wood with creamy yellow covers. The chairs in the room were placed in a circle around Kurt. Widow Swanson, Frank Hansen, Hugo Friis, Federico Ruez, and Alessandra Chavez, sat in the other chairs.

"Before we begin ..." Kurt said.

He struck out his right arm against the door that Jarle, Anastasia, and Hugo had just come through. It was reopened, and in came a woman who looked like she was in her late twenties. She had black, shoulder-length hair with bangs. Her lips were large, and she had black pupils.

"I want to introduce Sara Sofia Ulo. She has been responsible for leading the investigation for the police. Some of you have probably met her already. She was gracious enough to bring a bunch of police officers here, in case any problems appeared along the way. Isn't that right, Sara?" Kurt asked.

Sara nodded.

"It was the least I could do," she said.

Kurt continued.

"As you know, I was contacted by Hugo Friis to solve the case of John Fredly's murder. Immediately, this was an extremely difficult case. John Fredly appeared to have been shot, but it was almost impossible to figure out who was responsible. The reason I initially became involved in the case was that the local police here are apparently corrupt as hell. Not so strange, perhaps, that they couldn't find any witnesses to the murder whatsoever, either in terms of recordings, people, or alarms that had gone off. Had it even happened?" Kurt asked.

He snorted.

"Oh well. It would turn out that, whether they did a good or miserable job, they were right in one thing: the killer was impossible to identify. My colleague Frank and I have tried. In turn, we interviewed each and every one of you, as well as everyone else who was present during dinner and at Huaca Pucllana before, during, and immediately after John was shot."

Kurt suddenly began to circle around the floor in front of everyone as he looked down.

"After we had finished, I came to a conclusion. This was an impossible case. Everyone involved had an alibi for the time period in question. Or they were seen by another person who could swear that the one they had seen hadn't killed John. Everyone but …" Kurt began.

He stopped as suddenly as he had begun and turned to the congregation.

"You, Alessandra Chavez," he continued.

Kurt's eyes narrowed like a hawk about to capture its prey and focused on the innocent dark-blue eyes of Alessandra Chavez.

She was aghast.

"What? It can't … I didn't murder John Fredly! He was my father," she said.

Kurt made a triumphant gesture with his index finger toward her.

"Ah! Finally, you admit it! So that's why you were in John's room that night when you were discovered by Hugo," Kurt said.

Alessandra sighed.

"Yes, that's right. But he didn't find me. He couldn't possibly have done that," she said.

"He knew it was only the two of you who had the key to the room. What were you really doing in there?" Kurt asked.

"You already know that very well," said Alessandra indignantly.

"I'd like to hear you say it and explain why you lied," Kurt said.

"I wanted DNA to make sure he was my dad. I ... couldn't take it up with him until I was sure. I hadn't known him that long, so I wasn't sure how he would react. And I just lied because I wanted to avoid being involved in this," said Alessandra.

"Well, you got involved. Still, it wasn't really your fault. It turned out that the killer was trying to get you involved," Kurt said indignantly.

"But who's the killer?" asked Alessandra.

"I'm coming that that," assured Kurt. "When I realized you were his daughter, I had to try to reconcile this with the fact that you had no alibi or anyone who could testify for you. I couldn't. It just didn't add up. But at last I realized to my dismay what an idiot I had been."

Now all the eyes in the room, including Frank's, were aimed at Kurt. He had started circling again and was once again reminiscent of a hawk that could attack at any time.

"I always assumed John didn't know he was your dad. This was what your mother told you, wasn't it?" Kurt asked.

Alessandra frowned.

"How did ..." said Alessandra.

"I want to hear you say it," Kurt said.

"Yes, that's right," said Alessandra.

"Exactly. That means she lied to both of us. She had to have had contact with John, at least just one-sided contact to say she had a child," Kurt said.

"But why would she lie about that?" Jarle protested.

"Maybe because she never received an answer," Kurt said. "This was at the beginning of John's career, and he couldn't afford to pay child support. But as his career progressed further and further ... Well, you can imagine. I hadn't had much contact with John after my studies ended, but I followed his career occasionally, and I read speculation that he was good for nearly a billion when he died. And this, as we say in news journalism, is where it starts to get interesting. Right, Frank?"

Frank nodded and smiled.

"Frank has recently lost his daughter in a car accident," Kurt said.

There was a gasp through the congregation.

"He was reasonably pissed at John. He couldn't grasp how he couldn't support his daughter if he knew he had one. And that made me think. The John I knew was a pretty nice guy. Admittedly, I think he must have been a hard businessman to have managed to earn a fortune close to a billion kroner, but he took care of those around him. He often spent money on his friends if they had no money, and before he died he had bought and restored a house in Holmenkollen for his parents. At this point, I started reviewing the motives of all those involved again, to make sure I hadn't overlooked anything," Kurt said.

Everyone in the room looked around nervously at each other.

"You," he said, pointing to Jarle, "hated him because he wouldn't sell the paintings to you."

"Hate is a strong word. God, I didn't want to kill the man," Jarle said.

"And you," he said, pointing to Anastasia. "You hated him because he didn't want you."

Anastasia gasped. Jarle looked furiously from her to Kurt before he hit her so hard that her body ended up on the floor.

"Sara Sofia," Kurt shouted.

He hadn't noticed that she had already thrown herself

over Jarle. A walkie-talkie call later, a man clad in all black and woman with a Peruvian appearance immediately came through a door and assisted her. Frank had already rushed to Anastasia.

"Is she alright?" Kurt asked.

"I'm fine. You monster, how could you!" she screamed.

Kurt snorted.

"I did you a favor. Have you heard of Stockholm Syndrome? I'm guessing it's not the first time he's hit you. In fact, I know. When you hugged me when I came to interview you, the cream on your skin spread onto my cheek and revealed a small portion of a bruise. Besides, what could a naturally beautiful woman like you want with so much makeup? Dear, the whole bathroom was overflowing with it. Not to mention that you were so easily charmed by Karl Homme. But when I was told by Hugo that John had received several love letters signed "A," I put two and two together. You were never interested in Karl Homme, were you? He was just a tool to make John jealous. You couldn't do that, but what you did achieve was to make Jarle furious. Oh, he must have beat you black and blue that night John was murdered. Dear, please, turn him in," Kurt said.

Anastasia got up and revealed that she was bleeding heavily from her nose as the guards went out with Jarle secured in handcuffs.

"Frank, can you take care of her?" Kurt asked.

"Certainly," Frank said, grabbing her arm.

She reluctantly followed him out of the room.

"You," Kurt said, pointing to chef Federico Ruez. "You! You hated him because he paid you poorly and forced you to work extreme shifts. Why didn't you just leave?"

"I had no choice," Federico replied. "No one hires anyone with a criminal record."

"Exactly. I researched you a little. It was hard for me to believe that your nose was broken due to an accident at work. You told me you worked at Central Restaurante. But you said you were fired because you had been coming in late. It seemed unlikely. Why would a chef with a broken nose be fired because he was coming in late? That's why I went to Central Restaurante and talked to your former boss. She told me that you had a drug problem. That's why you were fired, and that is why you became a dealer on the street, right? And when you got out of prison, you were a broke, former chef who now had a broken nose. But John was there to welcome you," Kurt said.

"Some reception! That pig just wanted a cheap cook who did everything he asked," Federico said.

"But did that mean he deserved to die?" Kurt asked.

"Oh, he definitely deserved to die. But I didn't do it, I could never kill another human," Federico said.

"Well, I'm coming back to just that," Kurt replied.

Kurt hopped over to Mrs. Swanson and looked down at her. She seemed sunken, almost disappearing into her own body, when he looked at her. He assumed that the whole ordeal had made an impression on her. She wore a black dress, which was a stark contrast to her large, green eyes. Her red hair was tied in a tight knot at the back of her head under a wide, black hat.

"Mrs. Swanson, I didn't know anything about you until John introduced you to me. He said you were a tax refugee from England," Kurt said.

"Yes," she said, bewildered. "Is there anything wrong with that?"

"Not really," noted Kurt. "The problem was just that you owed millions of pounds to the British state. A friend of mine works in the tax administration over there and could confirm my suspicion. You were extremely interested in the paintings, weren't you? You knew they could solve all your financial problems. And you even admitted that you are gravely ill ... the idea of spending the last few years of your life in prison for crime could not have been so tempting. So, when you were contacted by those who were planning to steal the paintings, there was only one problem: you couldn't pay them."

"Steal the paintings? I have no idea what you're talking about, Mr. Hammer."

"Don't pretend. I will promptly reveal who wanted to steal the paintings, so you might as well confess," Kurt said.

"I didn't kill John Fredly," she said indignantly.

"No, but you might as well have. When you realized you couldn't pay for the paintings, you decided to blackmail John. You offered to reveal who you had been contacted by in exchange for one of the paintings," Kurt said.

"John was a stubborn bastard. He invited me to his dinner to show that he absolutely didn't care about the threat. He should have been more careful," the widow finally said.

"And you should have been more merciful," cried Kurt.

He closed his eyes for a few seconds before continuing.

"At this point ..." He took a break for effect. "It's the right time to take a moment to look at Karl Homme's murder. I had a theory about who had committed the murder, and I realized quite quickly that it was a murder that was done to scare me. But there wasn't a breakthrough in the case until I had left the scene and Sara Sofia decided to go back and look again. Maybe you should explain, Sara," Kurt said.

"Certainly," she said and entered the center of the circle with Kurt.

"When I talked to the Dazzler Hotel receptionist, there

was one thing I noticed. He had seen someone go in but didn't notice anyone going out. That would mean that either the killers had found a secret exit, or they were still in the hotel. So, I went through all the rooms on the same floor as Karl Homme's room. And sure enough, only two room numbers further down I found a room rented in the name of Alessandra Chavez. Ironically, I also found a blonde wig and a dress," Sara Sofia said.

"I had a theory that the killer would implicate Alessandra Chavez. And I had now confirmed that," Kurt said.

Then he turned around.

"This brings us to you," Kurt said, pointing to Hugo.

Hugo gave Kurt an indignant look.

"Me?! It was I who hired you! I haven't done anything! Besides, I'm too old to play Alessandra," Hugo said.

"Shut up and listen," Kurt said. "You were John's most trusted staff. It was only you who knew that he had recently changed his will, isn't that right?"

Hugo went pale.

"Huh? How did you know?" Hugo asked.

"I was just about to explain. I have cooperated a little with Aftenbladet at home in Norway, where I am employed. A colleague of mine, Felicia Alvdal, visited John's lawyer in Oslo for me to confirm my suspicions. Lawyers are hard nuts, unfortunately. He didn't want to, or couldn't, say anything about whom or what the changes concerned, but he could confirm that changes had been made. Specifically, just a few weeks before John died. Isn't it true that John had transferred his entire fortune to Alessandra?" Kurt asked.

"You can't prove that," cried Hugo.

"I just want to hear you say it," Kurt said.

"Well, I can say so, because that's true. John had transferred his entire fortune to Alessandra just before he died," Hugo shouted.

"And isn't it correct, Hugo, that the fortune was previously dedicated to you?" Kurt asked.

Hugo sighed. "That's right," he said.

"Well, well, then we've got the facts on the table," Kurt said.

"We haven't," Hugo protested.

"Shut up," Kurt said.

He walked over to Alessandra, looked her in her eyes, and took the rose out from his breast pocket.

"Your father loved you," he said, giving it to her.

Alessandra began to cry quietly and cautiously.

"Thank you," she said.

Kurt jumped back to where he had stood and fished out a pack of Marlboro Gold cigarettes from his breast pocket. He leaned against a wall, opened it, pulled out a cigarette, and took out a lighter from his pocket and lit it. Then he put the lighter back in his pocket and pulled out an envelope from his other pocket. He held it up in front of the assembly. It was addressed to him, and the sender was lawyer John Christian Elden in Oslo.

"Now that John is buried, Mr. Elden could reveal the details of the will. And it turns out ... does anyone have a letter opener?" he said, looking over the group.

"I do," said Mrs. Swanson. She opened her black purse and pulled out a silver letter knife.

"Ah, good, good," Kurt said.

Kurt approached her and, picked up the knife, before returning and opening the letter.

"I can confirm that the deceased, John Fredly, changed his will two weeks before he died. His entire fortune, shareholdings, and all his directorships are left to his daughter, Alessandra Chavez. She could appoint a deputy to the board if it turned out that she didn't want the positions or needed time to decide," Kurt read. "The letter is signed by John Christian Elden."

"Why should I kill him because he changed the will? I wouldn't get any money anyway," Hugo said dryly.

"Ah, but that's what's so interesting. Because you would! Besides John, you were the only one who knew the code to the safe with the paintings. When I asked you if I could look at the pictures in the safe, you imagined that John had told you that the code should only be given to the heir. So, now that we've gotten to know who the heir is ..." Kurt took an extended pull of his cigarette. "Did you get a code for the safe from Hugo?" Kurt asked and approached Alessandra.

"No, never," said Alessandra.

"Exactly, that's what I thought," Kurt said.

"It proves nothing," Hugo protested.

"Shut up," cried Kurt.

He continued.

"John wasn't stupid. He knew someone else should have the code in case something happened to him. Well, you were the only one except for John Christian Elden. But John couldn't have predicted that the person he trusted over everyone else, his most trusted employee, would be the reason for his own downfall. That's why you bet that Alessandra would be arrested and that you would get the paintings before Elden got hold of them. After all, he lives in Norway. You and Federico Ruez struck a deal with Jarle, didn't you? You would sell the paintings to him, and then you could share the profits between the both of you. Not a billion, but nearly thirty million is no small profit, either. With John out of the way, you were the only one in Peru who could get into the safe, giving you plenty of time to take the paintings and replace them with copies," Kurt said triumphantly.

"Me!" exclaimed Federico indignantly. "Me?! How do you think we committed this murder, then?" he asked.

"Ah! That wasn't easy to figure out. When I realized how easy the whole murder was, I realized at the same time that I had been an idiot. The plan was so simple, yes almost banal that it was brilliant. One of you got hold of poison hemlock," Kurt said. "I suppose you put it in his food, Federico. Then Hugo served it, simply. One of the main symptoms of the plant poison hemlock is paralysis. It explains how John could fall from the top of the pyramid and apparently be dead when he hit me. And worst of all: there is no antidote! As soon as John had eaten his food, his fate was sealed," Kurt said.

"You beast," screamed Alessandra and threw herself at Hugo, who sat right opposite her. "How could you?" she shouted.

His chair rolled over so that he landed on the floor. She had his neck in a vise grip when Kurt had to throw one of his crutches and use all the power of his long body to pull her away.

"There, there. Don't give him that pleasure," Kurt said, holding her in his strong arms.

When she'd calmed down and gotten back to her place, Kurt bent down, picked up the crutch from the floor, and continued his explanation.

"So far, there was only one problem with my theory: it established motives, but I had no evidence. So, I made the family pay a private company in Lima to look at a sample and quite rightly. His blood contained traces of poison hemlock. Which of you got the plant?" Kurt asked.

"It was me. I got it shipped from Europe," replied Federico Ruez.

"You damn idiot," cried Hugo Friis.

"We might as well give up! He's caught up with us. But I would like to know how you found out that he hadn't been shot," Federico asked.

"Ah, good question! But first I want to know how you killed Karl Homme," Kurt replied.

"I choked him. Early in the morning, I had checked into a room on another floor as myself. Then I left the hotel as myself and checked in as Alessandra. I left the hotel as Alessandra and came back a little later, hoping the evening attendant would have gone home. Later in the day, I left the hotel again as myself," Federico said.

Kurt palmed his face so hard that it sounded like he could have crushed his nose.

"But you hadn't counted on Sara Sofia's steadfastness. How did you know Karl had called me?" Kurt asked.

"Easy. He called me and said it quite simply. Hugo made him believe he could get a percentage of the money if he helped get you out of the way. But that idiot was too softhearted. He was going to crack and therefore he had to pay with his life. When you showed up with a hotel employee, I wasn't willing to take that risk," Federico replied.

"How did you know I had an employee with me?" Kurt asked.

"I had taped a small microphone on the ceiling in the hallway," Federico replied.

"And when you didn't take care of me in the hotel room, you called Hugo ..." Kurt said.

"Who engaged two murderers on motorbikes. That's right," Federico said.

"Well, you almost managed to take my life. But not quite," said Kurt triumphantly.

Federico snorted.

"How did you know that John hadn't been shot?" asked Federico.

"Well, neither I nor the forensic examiner could recognize John's wound as a gunshot wound. I would suggest that it might have come from a potato peeler or the like. Besides, the one who struck John hit him in the chest, just below the heart. When the forensic examiner, Alejandro, eventually looked at John, he never found any bullet. That was when I realized something was wrong. There was never an exit hole, and the bullet could not have disappeared by itself," Kurt said.

"So who struck John?" asked Alessandra with horror.

"Well, it's pretty obvious, isn't it? The one who had the opportunity and motive was Jarle Sørdalen. He stood on top of the pyramid as John was on his way up. He himself said he was wearing gloves all the time because he had mysophobia. That is, phobia of bacteria, correct? But when he got out of the bathroom in his room with Anastasia, he didn't take the time to wash his hands! The door to the bedroom was open, and Frank and I could hear that Anastasia was being beaten. That was when I realized that he was wearing gloves for a different reason. A person with a mysophobia would never have left a bathroom with a toilet without washing their hands once or twice. Because he was wearing gloves, he wouldn't have left any DNA traces as he struck John. Still, Alejandro discovered some small hairs near John's wound, and I'm betting that if the police compare them to Jarle's hair, they'll realize it's his," Kurt replied.

Kurt sighed.

"There's just one thing I don't understand. Why would you hire me to solve the case?" Kurt said.

"Well, it would look a little strange if I, the closest coworker, didn't engage anyone to resolve the matter, wouldn't it? Of course, I didn't think you would be capable. Anyway, John deserved to die. I had worked for him for over twenty years, and he had already promised me his inheritance. Then that damn whore came into the picture," Hugo said and spat in the direction of Alessandra.

Hugo pulled a revolver out of his pocket and aimed it at Alessandra.

"I wouldn't do that if I were you. The whole house is surrounded. You won't get away," Kurt said.

"Well, then it doesn't matter if she dies," Hugo said, then smiled and stood up. He walked slowly toward Alessandra with the gun poised.

Just as he had placed himself behind Alessandra with his gun to her back, four police officers came rushing in through the door across the room. They were followed by Sara Sofia. All of them lifted their guns out of their holsters and directed them towards Hugo when they saw what was going on.

"Hugo Friis! Drop your weapon, you're surrounded," the oldest policeman said.

As he said it, Hugo Friis, trembling, took his weapon and aimed it at his mouth.

"No," cried Kurt and threw himself over him. When he hit Hugo, the revolver went off.

A sound like a thunderbolt went through the whole room as a shot was loosed in the direction of Sara Sofia.

She screamed and cursed as her body shook and she fell backward. Two policemen threw themselves over Hugo, while the third stood behind Federico Ruez and chained his arms behind his back with handcuffs.

Kurt groped around on the floor, eventually gathered his crutches, got up, and put one arm around Alessandra.

"I'm alright. Call for an ambulance," she cried desperately.

Kurt took out his cell phone and dialed the ambulance.

Federico Ruez reluctantly followed the police out of the room while Hugo had to be dragged by two policemen. Alessandra walked over to Sara Sofia and removed the woman's shirt before tightening it around her leg.

"Lo siento, todo esto es mi error," mumbled Alessandra. *Sorry, all this is my fault.*

"No, I did my job," replied Sara Sofia.

Ten minutes later she was put on a stretcher and carried out of the room.

Frank returned. "Jarle is arrested, suspected of domestic violence and conspiracy to murder. I made her confess," he said proudly.

"Thank goodness," Kurt and Alessandra answered in chorus.

"So," Frank said. "Are we going to celebrate without alcohol? That the case is solved?"

Kurt waved a forefinger against him. "A good friend of mine is still dead. If anything, we should drink to his memory," Kurt said.

"Alright with me, as long as we don't get stupid drunk," Frank said.

"That sounds like a date! Alessandra, would you like to join?" Kurt asked.

"Thanks for thinking of me, but I've had enough excitement for a day. I think it's time for me to start packing to leave the house and start thinking about whether I want to continue in Dad's line of work. Easier said than done ... " she said.

Kurt sighed.

"I wish I could help you," he said.

"Thank you," said Alessandra before she came over and kissed him on the cheek.

"I have a favor to ask of you. When I took the case, I did it against the doctor's recommendation—I really came here to relax, and Hugo promised that he would try to get me money. I'm in a small financial crisis," Kurt said.

"How much do you need?" asked Alessandra.

"Thirty-seven thousand," replied Kurt.

"Send me your account number and consider it done," said Alessandra.

Kurt smiled.

"You're your father's daughter," Kurt said.

"What do you mean?" asked Alessandra.

"He always bought beer for anyone who wanted it," Kurt said with a small laugh.

"Can I ask you for a small favor?" Alessandra asked.

"Of course," Kurt replied.

"If I fly you down here, could you set aside a day or two to tell me about Dad? I didn't know him," said Alessandra.

Kurt looked at her and gave her a long and heartfelt hug.

"You should go to Norway and talk to Jonas and Linn as well," Kurt said.

"I've agreed to come to Grandma's funeral. I'm looking forward to seeing Norway," said Alessandra and smiled.

An hour later, Kurt and Frank found themselves in the English bar, the Old Pub, where the smell of dark beer hung in the air and flags from all the countries in the world adorned the ceiling.

"You know you only have indications that Federico is involved, right?" Frank noted.

He had just bought an English, dark, mild ale and promised extensively and sacredly that it would be the only alcohol he consumed that evening. They stood by the bar counter.

Shouldn't, should, shouldn't ... thought Kurt as the taste of hops and malt appeared on his tongue and made cold sweat appear on his lower back.

Kurt lifted his eyes and saw the Norwegian flag on the roof.

I'm going home. Felicia is waiting for me, he thought, ordering a diet cola.

"I know, but I gambled that he would admit that he had done it if I explained what had happened," Kurt replied.

"Cheers for John Fredly," Frank said, lifting his glass.

"Cheers. Tonight, I'll sleep with a clear conscience," Kurt said, smiling.

EPILOGUE
AUGUST 5, 2014

Kurt had promised himself that he would visit Sara Sofia Ulo before returning home to Norway. He found her in a single room at Clinica Javier Pardo, a concrete colossus dressed in white tiles and inserted with the initials "CJP" at the very top in blue letters.

"Hey," he said.

She was lying in a room that was barely big enough to accommodate the bed she was lying in. The walls and tiles on the floor were like snow. The ceiling was painted sky-blue. If it hadn't been for the smell of disinfectant and spirits in the air, Kurt could have sworn that he was suddenly in a completely different season.

Sara Sofia's long, black hair was tied in a knot at the back of her head. Large bags under her eyes made her pupils appear blacker than usual. The scar across her right eye looked longer than he had seen it before. Her big lips were somehow swollen, and Kurt thought she looked like a boxer who had just come out of the ring.

He walked over to her and gave her a hug and a pile of roses he had bought on the side of the road.

"Are you ok?"

"The doctors have assured me I'm going to survive, in any case. They had to remove a good deal of my liver. I suppose that's a sign that I should stop drinking," she said.

Kurt wasn't sure if she was sarcastic or not, her voice somewhat mushy. It came out of her like frost smoke in the winter in Siberia. *She's probably high on morphine,* Kurt thought.

"Thank you so much for the flowers," she said, smiling.

"My pleasure. I had a debt to pay to John, and I wouldn't be able to forgive myself if it had hurt you ... I'm sorry I sent you here," Kurt said.

"My God, yesterday it was Alessandra and now you. It was my choice to become a police officer. You know what I was thinking right after I was shot yesterday?" Sara Sofia asked.

"Let's hear it," Kurt said.

"Better me than you or Alessandra," said Sara Sofia.

"Why didn't you put on protection?" Kurt asked.

"Rookie mistake. I'm expecting the boss up any moment. He'll give me a real overhaul. Hadn't imagined that Hugo was going to carry a gun, but now I've learned. When are you going home?" asked Sofia.

"Rookie mistake? I never actually asked you how you got your scar. I figured you had it from a similar situation. I'm going home today, actually. But I had to stop by to see you first," Kurt said.

"The scar is from my mother. She made me want to be a police officer. I moved away from home when I was sixteen, but I really don't like talking about it," Sara Sofia said.

Her eyes narrowed to two black slits in her wild face.

"You have someone at home, don't you?" asked Sara Sofia.

"How did you know?" Kurt asked.

"It was just a feeling I got when we woke up together. You had a guilty conscience written all over you," Sara Sofia replied.

"Was it that obvious?" Kurt asked.

"She's lucky to have you," Sara Sofia said.

She got up carefully, as if in slow motion, and kissed him on the cheek.

"Thanks. I think I'm lucky to have her, too," Kurt said.

"Now you have to go. I need to sleep," Sara Sofia said.

"I actually have a taxi waiting for me outside. Get well soon," Kurt said.

Sara Sofia had already closed her eyes and collapsed on her pillow.

Kurt kissed her on the cheek and left the room.

As usual when he landed at Værnes, Kurt Hammer had the feeling that the plane would crash into the ground. *Luckily, there was only turbulence this time,* he thought, relieved, as he stepped out of the plane and was greeted by a downpour so heavy that he wondered whether he had come to Bergen and not Trondheim.

"Have you missed it?" he asked Frank.

"Right now, I miss Alex most. I hope she is healthy enough to welcome me," Frank said.

"Is she awake?" Kurt asked as they stood in the passport queue.

"I got a message from my mother-in-law that she is, yes. Don't think she wanted to call me because she didn't know what mood I would be in," Frank said.

"Oh, how great," Kurt said.

The passport controller, a blonde with a side-cut and overly large earrings that looked as if she could be in her mid-twenties, winked at him.

"Welcome back to Norway, Mr. Hammer."

"Thanks," he said, smiling slightly.

Having picked up his luggage, he checked his mobile. Still no response from Felicia to the messages he sent from Amsterdam.

I can only hope that she is home, he thought, looking at the clock.

"Bye, Frank. The funeral will be next week, right?" Kurt said, giving him a hug.

"Most likely. I'll let you know," replied Frank.

A little past four. Felicia should be finished at work now, thought Kurt. He went downstairs, onto the street and into a taxi.

"Where are you going?" asked the driver.

He was a middle-aged Somali with a highly developed North-Trønder accent.

"Fjordgata 16," replied Kurt.

"Come from afar?" asked the man, looking in the mirror.

"Lima. I was there to get rid of the alcohol and ended up losing a good friend, as well," Kurt said.

"Sorry," the man said.

"No problem. I owed him a favor and paid my debt," Kurt said.

Outside Fjordgata 16, he dialed Felicia's number. After a few minutes, she finally answered.

"Hi, Kurt. Sorry, my mobile wasn't charged. Where are you now?" she asked.

"I'm standing outside," replied Kurt.

"You better come up, then," she said.

Felicia's apartment wasn't great, but Kurt thought it was nice.

The walls were painted white, and the floor consisted of light brown parquet. The kitchen was completely white except for a metal gray microwave.

"Hey," Felicia said as Kurt came up.

Her icy-blue eyes stared at him with a mixture of fear and longing.

She hugged him. Kurt let his fingers slide gently through her dark brown hair that had grown almost to her waist. He had completely forgotten how much he missed the smell of Chanel No. 5, which crept out of every pore of her body.

Felicia had put Miles Davis's "Kind of Blue" on the record player under the TV. The long trumpet tones mingled with the sound of raindrops hammering on the window panes.

"It's ... good to have you back," she said and looked shyly down at the floor.

"Are we going to sit down? We have to talk," Kurt said.

"Let's do that," she said.

They sat on a gray sofa in front of the TV.

"I ..." they said at the same time.

"You first," Felicia said.

"The first night in Lima, I woke up with a police investigator in bed. Neither I nor she knows if we had sex. We both had too much to drink," Kurt said and sighed.

Felicia did not move a muscle.

"Do you remember when I called you to ask where you would drink if you were Frank?" she asked.

"Yes," replied Kurt.

"I found Frank at Olav's pub. He was completely crushed and had already started drinking when I got there.

We were both drunk, and that night I kissed him," Felicia said.

"I figured. I was pissed off, but when I realized he had lost Stine, it was as if that kiss never happened," Kurt said.

"So, where are we in all this mess?" asked Felicia.

"We?" Kurt asked.

"Yes, we, as in us," replied Felicia.

"Well, when I woke up after the first bullet in Lima, I realized what I was about to lose. I haven't tasted alcohol after that. I love you, Felicia," Kurt said.

Felicia smiled.

"I've missed you," she said.

She leaned against him and kissed him fervently for a long while to the sound of the Miles Davis's trumpet.

On the other side of the city, Frank gently knocked on the door to room 456 in St. Olav's hospital. He was stopped by a middle-aged doctor with Eastern European features, sleepy eyes, and a great mustache.

"Hi, I'm Doctor Polskaya. I am the one responsible for your wife now. I don't know if you remember me," he said.

"You were in charge of Olya, weren't you?" Frank asked.

"That's right. The thing is, right now ..." Polskaya replied.

He looked down at the floor.

"We should go sit down," he said.

"It's fine, I can stand," Frank said.

"Alexandra just woke up from a coma less than twenty-four hours ago," Polskaya said.

"I know," Frank said.

"We are uncertain about her condition and how much she actually remembers. Therefore, we haven't told her that Stine is dead," Polskaya said.

Frank didn't move a muscle.

"I know it's hard to fathom, but it was important that you know before seeing her again," he said.

"I ... thank you," Frank said.

"Just call me if anything comes up. Here's my card," Polskaya said, giving Frank a card he pulled up from his breast pocket.

Frank nodded, turned around resolutely, and knocked on the door.

"Come in," he heard from inside.

When he entered the room, Frank had to pull himself together in order not to cry.

Alexandra's blond hair was tied in a knot at the back of her head. Some of the ends were still bloody, and her head was held up by a neck collar. Her left eye had swollen to the size of a medium tomato, and her right leg hung in straps from the ceiling.

Grete, Alexandra's mother, sat in a chair next to the bed and looked worried about her daughter. It looked like Grete hadn't slept for several days.

Frank walked over to Alexandra, stroking a couple of hairs off her forehead and kissing her tenderly.

"How are you?" was all he could say.

"All things considered, I'm alright," she replied.

Oh my God. Her voice ... She must be as high as a Christmas tree, he thought and shuddered.

"Will you be able to walk again?" Frank asked.

"The doctors say they're not sure. Fortunately, only one of my legs got the brunt of it. How's Stine doing?" she said.

"She's doing ... I think she's doing well," Frank stammered.

Immediately, he got up.

"Maybe it's good for you to get some rest? I just returned home from Peru and need to rest," he said apologetically.

"Yes, that's probably wise," Alexandra said and yawned.

Frank gave Grete a worried look but realized that he was unable to relieve her now.

"I'll be back tomorrow," Frank said, kissing Alexandra on her mouth.

Having closed the door to the room, he turned around and proceeded with determined steps towards the nearest exit.

Frank didn't stop walking until he had come to Brukbar twenty minutes later, next to Trøndelag Theater. He thrived here and occasionally went in and grabbed a beer after reviewing performances in the theater.

"Nice weather out, huh?" noted the bartender as Frank entered, dripping wet from head to toe. He sat down by the open glass façade, beneath a giant chandelier shaped like a ball.

"A Dahls," Frank said, putting his head in his hands.

<<<<>>>>

THANKS

First and foremost, thanks again to Ida Elise Østberg. She was a big help on the first book in this series. Getting to work with her again was a real pleasure – few things can match being able to scream with joy because you realize, after almost three years spent writing, you've done something right when your first reader gives you wonderful feedback.

Secondly, a huge thank you to all employees at Starbucks in Neumannsgate 25 og Vetrlidsallmenningen 2 in Bergen. I've been sitting day and night, occupying ungodly amounts of space, as I've written and written. If there's been few people, I've been served coffee in my seat – thanks so much, I love you guys! I'd also like to give thanks to all the employees at the newly opened Starbucks in Kristiansand!

Third, I'd like to give thanks to employees at other Starbucks cafes I've visited around the world while writing this book. Of course, the cafe in Lima, Peru, but also in London, Wien and St. Petersburg.

Last, but not least: a great thanks to my American

editor, Maxann Dobson, who's surpassed all my expectations. Both the Norwegian and English version of the book are much better thanks to her!

Dear reader,

We hope you enjoyed reading *Murder In Lima*. Please take a moment to leave a review, even if it's a short one. Your opinion is important to us.

Discover more books by Mats Vederhus at https://www.nextchapter.pub/authors/mats-vederhus

Want to know when one of our books is free or discounted? Join the newsletter at http://eepurl.com/bqqB3H

Best regards,

Mats Vederhus and the Next Chapter team

You might also like:

A Mersey Killing by Brian L Porter

To read the first chapter for free go to:
https://www.nextchapter.pub/books/mersey-killing-british-crime-mystery

Lightning Source UK Ltd.
Milton Keynes UK
UKHW020318270221
379474UK00010B/578/J